THE VIRUS

The Virus

House of Heaventree
Book 2

NICOLE SEITZ

Water Books

Copyright © 2022 by Nicole Seitz

All rights reserved. No part of this book may be reproduced in any manner whatsoever without written permission except in the case of brief quotations embodied in critical articles and reviews.

First Printing, 2022

ADVANCE PRAISE

"A suspenseful, imaginative, page-turner, set in a modern-day dystopian world where a brother-sister duo must rely on the power of their biblical faith and a secret society to survive. Nicole Seitz's first YA Christian fiction series is a captivating, fast-paced read that leaves readers wanting to know when the next book is coming out." - **Angela May**, *NY Times* bestselling co-author of *The Islanders*

"Fast-paced and hard to put down, THE VIRUS boils with action and suspense. Great character development and deeply rooted Christian values make this a wonderful YA or Middle Grade read." - **J.E. Thompson**, author of *The Girl at Felony Bay* and *Buccaneer's Spit: A Race for the Treasure*

"Seitz handles the work's straightforward Christian allegory with enough skill and energy to head off any predictability. The interplay between the Flanagan children and their schoolmates at Heaventree is well rendered, and...Seitz manages to create a good balance between the Christian subtext and the bleak future setting. Religious readers are likely to find this work congenial and faith-affirming." - ***Kirkus Reviews***

"Incredible suspense that drew me to the end in one sitting. One. It reads like both breaking news and a timely warning." - **Shellie Rushing Tomlinson**, author of *Seizing the Good Life*

"Concise and intense with religious scripture woven into the story, this novel is both suspenseful and engaging. Seitz creates a realistic and frightening story full of finely articulated ideas....a rich and original work that is prophetic in nature." - ***The BookLife Prize***

For those who overcome.

~ 1 ~

When the sun rises over the lake at Heaventree, Flare and Cornelius Flanagan have already been awake for hours, imagining the reactions of their friends when they learn the news: the world outside their walls is at war. Everyone they left behind is in danger.

They sit on the cool grass, arms on knees, watching the ripples slowly circle out from tiny movements beneath the surface of the water. There isn't a word between them, only tense silence. They're both thinking about their own parents, too, praying they are safe somehow. Somewhere.

The campus of Heaventree is dotted with new houses, and the scent of sawdust still wafts by every now and again. It's not an unpleasant smell. The Houses of Heaventree were built by hand by students in six days. Although Cornelius' body is still sore and Flare's arm still broken, they each feel a strange sense of accomplishment, seeing the houses all lined up, soldiers in waiting.

They did that.

"Good morning, Heaventree!" Mr. Deal's voice bellows over the loudspeakers, jolting the teens. "Rise to a new day, my friends. Come, let us fill our bellies and our souls with a very special breakfast. You don't want to miss it. See you in the Main Hall. Le-et's go!"

Flare and Cornelius stay put. Over the next ten minutes they watch their friends straggle bleary-eyed into the Main Hall and line up behind the buffet. From where they are sitting, they can see clearly through the large windows as the tables begin to fill up. Neither is eager to join them.

"I guess we gotta go in," says Flare.

"I can't eat," says Cornelius.

"Me neither, but we're gonna have to force it down. Who knows what we'll have to do today." Flare turns to Cornelius and grabs the top of his hand. "Promise me you'll eat. Fill your pockets if you have to."

Okay," he says. "Promise."

The sunlight spreads a little more, and they turn one last time toward the six Houses of Heaventree. No more hammering. No more bustle of kids running here and there in a frenzy of construction and confusion.

"Hard to believe we did that in six days," says Flare. "Think of what this group is capable of. We totally underestimated ourselves."

"Yeah," says Cornelius. "But Deal didn't."

"Let's try to remember that," says Flare. "We have to trust he knows what he's doing. We really don't have a choice. You ready?"

"I guess."

They rise and brush the grass off their clothes. Flare picks pieces carefully off her cast on her right arm and touches the signatures of her friends there—Marcus, Josh, Nattie, Amy, Joe—then they head side by side into the building, solemnly steeling themselves.

"Whatever happens, be strong for Amy," says Cornelius in the doorway. He catches his sister's eye and holds it.

"You know I will," she says. "You be strong for Joe and for all the boys in your house. Goofy kids..."

Cornelius cracks a smile and nods. Then he sets his eyes on his table and goes in at full speed.

Joe grabs him as he passes by. "Dude, where were you?" he whispers.

"With Flare. I'll tell you soon. What is that? Pancakes?"

"Yeah, with bananas and cinnamon sugar," says Joe, stuffing a bite in his mouth in approval.

Cornelius grabs his plate and heads to the back of the line. Josh Dunwright is in front of him, broad shoulders blocking the view of the food.

"Hey, Corn, how's it going?" says Josh, just passing time.

"Good," says Cornelius. "You?"

"Tired," says Josh. "Can't believe we have to get up so early. I mean, even God rested on the seventh day. Am I right?"

Cornelius nods and looks around as he moves a little closer to the food. He fiddles with his plate.

"Look at them," says Josh. "All the mentors are so serious. It's not like they did a ton to help us this week. Right? Well, except for Coach Arnold. He's awesome. We're supposed to play some ball today. A reward, I guess."

Cornelius closes his eyes. He doesn't want Josh to see

the sadness. There won't be any basketball today. "They look tired, too," says Cornelius. "I imagine wrangling 144 teenagers into building six houses—"

"Barns," says Josh.

"Yeah, barns, but still, it couldn't have been easy."

"We could probably run things just as good," says Josh, beginning to add food to his plate. It looks like he's eating for two.

"Maybe," says Cornelius. "But I'm glad I'm not in charge." He moves to the other side of the buffet table and tries to quit the conversation.

After Cornelius has ingested as many pancakes as he can, someone clinks a glass with a spoon to get everyone's attention. He swallows hard. His heart starts racing wildly.

Joe takes a sip of his juice and turns around in his seat to face the mentors' table. Mr. Vollmer stands up.

"Friends," he says, "we want to take a moment to praise you, once again, for the hard work you put in this week. When we," he turns and lifts his hand, "your mentors, walk the grounds and inspect your houses that you built with your own hands and with your hearts and minds and souls, we are grateful. God provided you with strength, with wisdom, and in the end," he turns to look at Atlys and her table of girls, "with unity and heart for one another. I could not be more proud if you were my own children."

Mr. Vollmer chokes a little and turns to Mr. Deal who stands now.

"Yes, we are encouraged by what we saw this week. A group of 144 perfect strangers coming together as the body of Christ. We hope that these past few days, although difficult in many ways, have brought you each closer. Knitted your hearts together. I know I feel much closer to all of you now." He turns and looks toward Cornelius. He clears his throat.

"So, well. I guess this is enough praise for the day, except for the praise we owe our Father in heaven." Mr. Deal closes his eyes and bows his head. "Heavenly Father, God of all knowledge, we come before you of one heart and spirit today. Lord, we seek your guidance in the days to come. We seek your protection over every student here, over every teacher and staff member. We know that faith and perfect love drives out fear. And so this is our prayer. Let us not be afraid to do what you have called us to do. In Jesus' name we pray. Amen."

The room mumbles amens and begins to move.

"Hold on," says Mr. Deal. "Please. I'm afraid there's more. You see. Well...you may have noticed Miss Carmine, the mentor for the House of Flare, has been absent for the past few days." He looks toward Flare who covers her mouth with her hand. Amy and the other girls look at her, but she keeps her gaze on Mr. Deal.

"Well, we have some difficult news. Miss Carmine was injured...and...has died."

The room erupts with gasps and moans. Flare's tablemates grow still, their faces contorting in quiet anguish.

"What happened?" calls out Josh.

"What happened, well, there is more we need to tell you. I wish it weren't so but—"

"We're at war," says a mild-mannered Madame Dubose, standing now, as straight and as taut as she can.

"The world has become a very dangerous place for those of us without the mark," she says. "It is why you all were sent here. You may have read as much in your guardian's letters. But since you've been here, the Global Union has begun hunting down non-GUYs."

"Our parents?" calls out Nattie.

"It appears so. Anyone who is not connected to the G.O.D. is at risk. And...it seems that the pets—of all things—all pets are being targeted."

"But why? They're just animals!" says Nattie.

Mr. Deal stands again. This time the room grows so silent you could hear a pin drop.

"If you have ever had an animal as part of your family, you know the loyalty and love these creatures are capable of. It is these traits that are now being exploited. All pets are being chipped. They are having data downloaded just like their masters. Except for the pets of non-GUYs. These poor creatures are being confiscated so that they will, out of love and loyalty, lead the Global Union to their owners. Owners who are in hiding now."

Some of the teens are starting to cry, thinking of their families, of their pets and friends left at home.

"Today, we begin our new assignments. You will each be given tasks. These are serious assignments—every one is different, and each is essential. We are at war, friends, and as such, I expect each one of us to pull together in love and in sacrifice. We have much to do. We are running out of time. If any of you thinks he or she may not be up to the challenges that are coming, speak now."

He stops and looks around the room. The students

straighten up. One by one, they lift their heads. Cornelius stands. Then Flare, then each head of a house—Josh, Marcus, Nattie and Atlys. Their housemates join them until the room is filled with teens standing at attention.

It appears a unified House of Heaventree is ready to join the cause.

~ 2 ~

Cornelius and Joe lead the way into the house they built by hand, and the other boys in their group follow them in. It smells like fresh sawdust and pine, and a nice breeze enters with them. Mr. Deal comes in last and asks everyone to take a seat.

"Boys, now that the House of Flare has no mentor, I've asked the girls to join us here. Scooch over to make room for them, please."

As the girls trickle into the big empty room and head to the right, the boys move away like grease to water over to the other side. There are a few giggles and a couple of red faces in the process. Mr. Deal goes straight to the back and sits against the wall. He's in the twelve o'clock position to this circle of 48 teens.

Cornelius notices he seems weary, burdened.

"Hey guys, well, I guess we all know there is more to the story than we even knew a week ago," says Mr. Deal. "And this is exactly why this school is important. As believers, we must be ready for the unexpected. It's exactly what is expected of us. And it won't be easy. Jesus promised us we would have troubles. But he said something else too. Cornelius. Help us out?"

Cornelius lifts his head a little higher and says, "In this world you will have trouble. But take heart! For I have overcome the world. John 16:33."

"Indeed," says Mr. Deal. "You will have trouble. Not if. You will. BUT, Jesus says, take heart. Don't be afraid. Don't be alarmed. Why? Because He has already overcome the world. Any trouble you and I face...it pales in comparison with the battle that Jesus has already fought in the spiritual realm. In the end, it turns out okay for those who walk with him." He gets quiet. "In the end, it turns out well for those who endure. Those who overcome. Overcome what? Anyone?"

The room is quiet. Then Evan raises his hand. "Sir? We have to endure pain. Suffering. Worry. Doubt. We have to overcome temptations. Fears."

"Mister Chang, I could not have said it better myself. Did you guys think this last week was hard?"

The kids all talk at once, excitedly recalling their trials and triumphs. Finally, Mr. Deal says, "You know that was just preparation, right?"

Amy says, "We know, Mr. Deal. And we're ready. Just tell us what we need to do."

And so he begins to outline the tasks and the new teams that must form.

Cornelius, Marcus and Atlys are standing in a small wooden chapel. The beams in the ceiling are thick, and the pews hard and bare. The sweet odor of burning beeswax candles hangs around them.

Mr. Deal, Madame Dubose and Professor Moss come toward the three teens down the center aisle. "As you now know, you three have been tasked with rescue and reconnaissance," says Mr. Deal. "That means you must work together to rescue and bring back with you as many pets of non-GUYs that you can find."

"It also means you must bring back any information you can about what is happening on the outside," says Madame Dubose.

"You will be our spies," says Professor Moss, nodding at her protege, Atlys. "You will be our eyes and ears to the outside world."

"And because of all of this," Mr. Deal comes forward and puts his hand on Cornelius' shoulder, "you three will be in the most danger of any of us."

Cornelius' mind is spinning. His pulse is beginning to race. He looks around him. Is the chapel getting smaller? He holds his chest and tries to take a deep breath.

"We will cover you in prayer," says Madame Dubose. "And we will do more than this. Children, come closer..."

The three mentors put their hands on their students' heads. Then they begin to pray, softly at first and then louder. Soon a wind begins to swirl in the room and the candles blow out, sending wild smoke like flames all around them. Suddenly Marcus begins to pray along with them in some foreign language. Atlys reaches over and grabs Cornelius' arm and squeezes it, and he feels a peace come over him like he's never experienced before.

Everything is going to be okay. He knows it in his soul. He feels courage welling up within him. The prayer stops and the room falls completely silent. Cornelius stands up straight, takes a deep breath and with a knowing look to his mentor's eyes, says, "It's time then. Let's go."

Flare sits at her desk in her room in Chizoba Hall. Miss Carmine's notes are to the right of her sketchbook. She picks up a pen and prays. Then she stares at the blank page. She waits.

Waits.

Nothing.

Flare looks at the notes again.

Clear your mind of anything—no troubles, no worries, no cares. When we truly pray in the Spirit, we get out of the way, and the Spirit utters the prayers we cannot. The same goes for art. You must move out of the way. Don't give your drawing a thought. No objective critique—this is a good line, this one didn't work—none of it. This is the hardest part. You must move out of the way, remove everything you have learned. You have a gift. Remember that the gift is not your own, nor is it about you.

Flare closes her eyes and attempts to clear her mind. But she is thinking of Cornelius. *Where is he now? Is he in danger? No. Clear your mind. Cast your cares upon the Lord. Where were we? Oh yeah, mind-clearing.*

Flare opens her eyes and sets the pen on her paper in the center. She gives no thought as to what she will draw. She begins to move the pen, and a black line curves to the right and then down, now squiggly and then straight. She resists correcting it, resists turning it into anything representational. As her abstract line fills the page, she focuses on the Lord and begins to praise Him. She loses track of time, loses track of the line her hand is making and then sees the dome over Heaventree in her mind's eye. Flare can see where the cracks are. With everything she has in her, she begins to seal the cracks with her lines, mending and blending them until the dome is complete.

Or is it? Did she just imagine all that?

As if waking from sleep with her eyes open, Flare sees now the image that has emerged on the page. Instead of being an abstract scribble, it has taken form. She looks closely and is astounded. How did she draw that without knowing it? And how does it resemble them so well? Her heart races when she realizes—this drawing of Corn, Atlys and Marcus—it hasn't happened yet.

Flare grabs her sketchbook, closes it carefully, then sets out to find Mr. Deal. He has to see this. He has to tell her what it means.

~ 3 ~

Cornelius, Atlys and Marcus are headed back to the arched entry of Heaventree, their mentors trailing behind them. The three teens are loaded with heavy backpacks. Atlys' and Marcus' are filled with medicines, pet foods, leashes, muzzles and collapsible pet carriers. Cornelius' pack holds a compass, maps, flashlights and rations of food and water, enough to keep the three teens alive for a week. The packs are heavy now, but will only get lighter as their mission gets underway.

The three stop at the exit, their minds thick with thoughts.

Cornelius thinks of Flare. He told her goodbye, more like 'see you soon,' but still, knowing he is going out there to face God-knows-what and that Flare is staying here, following in the footsteps of Miss Carmine who lost her life doing her dangerous work—it's enough to fill his heart with worry.

Except…it's strange. This time he's not scared. He's not worried. His normal scaredy-cat self must be hiding in the shadows, because it's not here. Cornelius feels at peace. He doesn't feel invincible—that would be foolish. Instead, he knows he's in God's will. Danger or not, there is no safer place to be.

For a split second, Cornelius is tempted to turn around and look at the beautiful campus of Heaventree one last time, to remember it, to hold on to it, and maybe to catch a glimpse of his sister's or Amy's face. But he doesn't. The image of Lot's wife turning back to look at Sodom and then becoming a pillar of salt grips him. There's no turning back when he's heard the call of God.

It's time to leave. He's ready.

When the group passes the fig tree that marks the secret campus, its full leaves and branches wave in the wind.

"It's grown a lot in the last week," says Atlys. The group remains silent, each knowing what this means, that this tree, this sign of the times, is speaking its truth—that the end of times is even nearer.

At the entrance to the tunnel, Mr. Deal stops them and says, "This is where we must leave you folks. It's time for you to go on alone."

Madame Dubose takes hold of Marcus' arm and looks up into his dark eyes. "Trust that the Holy Spirit has filled you and can do things you, alone, cannot. Nothing will be the same out there. And you, in here," she touches his chest. "Nothing is the same in here either. The Spirit of God dwells here. Live freely, child."

Marcus hugs her, and the others hug their mentors. Professor Moss gives Atlys a knowing look and last smile. Mr. Deal folds his hands beneath his chin and looks intently at his protege. "Cornelius. I don't need to tell you what this means, how important your work is. The animals, they come first. Why? We don't need to know more than that right now. Just remember your mission and stay on task. Can you do that?"

Cornelius nods. Then he says, "Take care of Flare."

"Done," says Mr. Deal.

Then Cornelius, feeling much less anxious about this ride into the dark unknown than he did just a week ago, leads his group into a coal car, utters the words that start the wheels turning, and lifts his hand in a last wave goodbye without ever turning around.

In the pitch blackness of the tunnel, Cornelius, Marcus and Atlys feel the vibrations of the coal cars in their bodies as they roll over the tracks. Cornelius chooses to keep his eyes shut until they reach the end. He knows how long it will take, and it takes every ounce of energy to keep his mind at peace instead of giving in to claustrophobia. He won't let it overcome him this time.

"In Africa," says Marcus, leaning up to his ear from behind, "we have a saying. Where there is love, there is no darkness. There is light at the end of this tunnel, my friend."

Cornelius takes a deep breath and opens his eyes. He is glad that Marcus is with him. As for Atlys—he is having a harder time with his feelings about her. Part of him still doesn't trust her after how she acted during the building of their houses. But maybe she changed. Maybe she learned her lesson. He knows it's wrong to harbor ill feelings, and yet, there they are.

When the cars begin to slow down, Atlys shifts in the seat next to him. "Guess there's no turning back now," she says.

"Guess not," says Cornelius.

The three climb out of their coal cart and stand on shaky legs. They hoist their heavy packs on their backs and retrace the steps that brought them to Heaventree a week ago. When they arrive at the empty campus, they walk into the auditorium. "So strange to see all these empty seats," says Atlys.

The three climb up the stairs to the stage and turn to face the room. Cornelius can still hear Mr. Deal in his microphone as he announced them as leaders of their houses. He can still hear the chants of the crowd. How could it only be seven days ago that he and Flare left their parents? How will the boys in his house do while he's gone? Heat forms in the pit of his stomach, and he feels his pulse begin to race. "We've got to go now," says Cornelius. "There are people out there we've got to save."

"Animals, you mean," Atlys corrects him.

"Yes," says Cornelius, "but behind every pet is a human being. We save a pet, we save a human life."

"So let's be going now," says Marcus. Then he says loudly, "Very truly I tell you, you will see heaven open, and the angels of God ascending and descending on the Son of Man," and suddenly, the floor and ceiling begin to move and the three teens go up, up, up...

~ 4 ~

Flare is out of breath by the time she sees Mr. Deal in the distance. He is standing with Professor Moss and Madame Dubose under the shade of a tree. Is she too late? Did Corn leave already?

As she comes closer, drawing in hand, Mr. Deal turns and smiles.

"Well, here's our artist now. How goes it, Miss Flanagan?"

"Did they leave already? Is Cornelius gone?" she says.

"They left a few minutes ago, yes."

Silence surrounds as this sinks in for Flare. She puts her head down.

Madame Dubose reaches a frail arm over to her and touches Flare's back. "They are smart children, covered by the grace of our Lord. He will watch over them."

Flare nods. "I know He will, but...well, I tried it. I tried doing what Miss Carmine left in her notes, and it worked. Or at least I think it did."

"That's good news," says Professor Moss.

"Maybe," says Flare. "But something strange happened.

I could see the cracks in the dome somehow, and then...well then, I drew this."

She takes the drawing and hands it to Mr. Deal. He holds it and takes a slow deep breath. Then he passes it to Madame Dubose.

Mr. Deal turns around and seems to search the sky. When he comes back around, he has his arms crossed in front of him and a furrowed brow. "Flare, have you shown this to anyone else?"

"No," she says. "No one."

"It may mean something," he says, "or, it may not."

"But you think it does, don't you?"

Professor Moss holds the drawing in her hand and begins to fold it in half. "I am sure this drawing was nothing more than an overactive imagination," she says.

"But I wasn't even conscious—"

"I know," says Mr. Deal, taking Flare by the arm and beginning to move. "I think we ought to go check those notes and make sure nothing was left out. It could happen."

"But—"

Mr. Deal squeezes her arm to quiet her, and the two walk away from the other mentors and back toward the center of campus.

"Mr. Deal," says Flare. "I didn't make that up, I swear. I had no idea what I was even—"

"I know," he says. "And I believe you. It. I believe the drawing is real."

"But you said back there—"

"Flare, you must understand that people are just people. Saved or not, believers or not, humans are still human, and as such they—we—are subject to all sorts of failings. You were witness to it this week when Atlys didn't want to help your losing house."

"Yes, but this is different. This is so much worse! And if it's true, we've got to go warn them! Let me go after them."

"No," he says, firmly. "I will not put you in danger."

"But this was a prophecy, right? And you wouldn't have known about it if I hadn't shown you. You have to do something!"

"Something. Yes. But what, I am not sure of. I am also not sure of when. I need to get with the Lord on this. You're going to have to trust me."

"You've said that a lot," says Flare, stopping in the grass. "You've told me and Corn to trust you over and over, and now look at what's going on. You've sent him out there in a war. He's is danger. He's just a kid!"

Mr. Deal covers his face with his hands. Flare is not sure if he is praying or crying or what. Finally he says, "Flare, the danger your brother is in is real. For sure. But if what you're drawing shows comes true, then Atlys is in more danger. She's in danger of losing her very soul. And I had vowed not to lose any that the Lord has given me."

"So you'll do something?"

"Something, yes. As to what...I'm going to go figure that out now."

Mr. Deal leaves Flare's side and walks with purpose toward Castlebank. For a second she feels empathy for him. She can almost see the weight on his shoulders. She looks up and imagines the cracks in the invisible dome above her, and suddenly, she feels the weight of her own responsibility. She's going to need help—reinforcements. So she sets out to find the girls in the House of Flare.

~ 5 ~

Cornelius, Marcus and Atlys emerge onto Journey Street. They stand on the sidewalk next to Leaf Bookstore and Chang's Chinese Food. Across the street is a neon sign for Milo's Deli and Dry Cleaning, and at the intersection, a street lamp begins to flicker as dusk settles.

"Let's go," says Atlys. "We can't let anyone see us. We can't trust anyone."

"This way," says Cornelius. He knows this direction leads to his own street, his own house, and he longs desperately to go there, but he has a map. Each student at Heaventree was asked if they had left any pets behind, so this map covers quite a range—some not even in this state or country—but they have to start with the closest ones first. Since his dog, Pepper, died before he and Flare left home, there is no pet to rescue at his house. No reason to go there. Plus, his parents have probably gone into hiding. He hopes so, anyway.

It makes his heart hurt to think of them.

The three pull their caps down low over their heads and long bangs. They can't afford to let anyone see their foreheads that don't carry the mark of a GUY.

"It's too quiet," says Marcus. "There's a war going on, and I don't see anyone. I don't hear anything."

"Yeah," says Cornelius. "It's not what I thought we'd find either. Just blend in. Don't call attention."

As the three enter a neighborhood with matching houses and crisp, clean lawns, it's beginning to get a little darker, something that makes Cornelius feel better. More hidden.

Suddenly, he hears footsteps behind them. They are getting closer, harder. Cornelius turns his head slightly to catch a glimpse of the jogger as she runs by them.

"Whew!" says Atlys. "That scared me to death."

"Are we almost there?" says Marcus.

"Three more houses," says Cornelius. "That green one on the left."

It seems the next few steps are taking an eternity. Cornelius can feel his heart pounding in his chest. Does he have what it takes to be out here? What does he know? He has no special skills, no physical strength. Why in the world did Mr. Deal send him out here, anyway?

Cornelius is breathing heavy now and grabs at his throat. Suddenly, something hits his leg. He begins to cry out, but Marcus throws his hand over his mouth.

It's a dog. A curly black dog.

The three stare at the dog, but it stares back only into Cornelius' eyes. It is such a knowing look, that Cornelius wonders if it isn't the spirit of Pepper in there. It makes his heart race.

Marcus puts his hand down and pets its head. "This dog is scared."

"No collar?" asks Atlys.

"And no chip, either, not that I can see," says Marcus.

"Is this the pet we came for?" asks Atlys. "I thought we were looking for a Jack Russell Terrier."

"We are," says Cornelius. "I don't know who this one belongs to."

"Well, we have to help it," she says.

Cornelius motions to the other two to follow him quietly in between houses. The dog follows. Atlys grabs a handful of food from her pack and the black dog practically inhales it. "He's starving," she says. "He must be a good dog. Aren't you a good dog?"

"Shhhh," says Cornelius. "Get a leash. You stay here with him while we try to get inside."

Atlys slips a leash on the dog and sits down next to him. "Shhh, boy. Here." She gives him some more food, and Marcus and Cornelius turn the corner to the back of the house.

"See if anything is open," Cornelius whispers. The two boys check each door and window.

"Nothing," says Marcus.

"How are we going to get in? I don't know how to break into houses!" Cornelius feels his throat closing. And then he hears something.

Scratching.

The boys turn around and see a little dog standing at the back French door, peering out the bottom of the glass. He's panting, and it seems a struggle for him to lift his paw.

"Roger," says Marcus. "Hey, Roger." Marcus leans down

and puts his hand up on the glass. "We're going to get you out. Hold still. Cornelius, what now?"

Cornelius looks around. He sees a tree. Its branches curve near to an upstairs window. "Hold this."

Cornelius throws his pack down by Marcus and begins to climb the tree. When he gets to the top, he leans over to the window and presses upward. Nothing. He tries harder. Prays. Suddenly it opens. Cornelius awkwardly climbs inside and walks slowly through the house, taking care in case someone is there. There's an odor like stale dog pee, but it's not too bad. Perhaps the owners haven't been gone long. Why wouldn't they take their dog? He wonders. Maybe they didn't have time. In the kitchen, he sees a coffee pot half full and dishes still in the sink. The little dog wags his tail cautiously.

"It's okay, boy. We're here. We got you. You be quiet now, okay?"

The dog seems too tired to bark. Cornelius scoops him up in his arms and opens the back door. "I'll carry him," he says. When they see Atlys and the strange black dog, she reaches in her bag and gives the terrier some food.

But he barely eats.

"Hold on. He needs water. Check my pack."

Where is it?" asks Atlys.

"I left it with you, Marcus."

"I left it—"

The three stop in their tracks. Someone is coming on the other side of the house.

"In here!" The three teens and two dogs scramble behind the trash bins and huddle close. Cornelius can hear his own breathing. He prays that the dogs won't bark. *Please, God, keep us hidden.*

Cornelius is panic stricken but can't move. If someone gets hold of his backpack, then all their plans will be exposed! There's a map and addresses to all the houses!

They hear whistling and then it drifts off. The person is leaving. Cornelius waits for a minute to be sure the coast is clear and then hustles over to the back of the house. It's still there. The backpack is still there!

Thanking God under his breath, Cornelius hoists it up and onto his back, then goes to grab the others. Darkness has fallen. It's time to get them all to safety.

~ 6 ~

Flare finds Amy back in their room in Chizoba Hall. She's sitting on the edge of her bed, hugging her pillow.

"You okay?" asks Flare. She comes toward Amy and has a seat next to her.

"I guess," she says. "I just wish I knew what was going on with my parents."

The blow to Flare's gut is hard and unexpected. She knows the truth about Amy's parents. She knows they're dead. Their names are written in the Book of Martyrs. But she can't say anything. What good would it do to kill any hope Amy has for their survival?

Flare feels a twinge of guilt but thinks the Lord will understand. "It's awful not knowing. worrying about what might happen."

"The not knowing is the worst," says Amy.

"Is it?" asks Flare. She thinks of her own parents. She believes they are still alive. Well, she sort of knows it because their names haven't appeared in the Book, but still. Wouldn't she rather imagine them still living even if they weren't?

Wait a minute. It's been a while since she checked the

book. Flare feels like she might throw up. "What's that?" she says, hoping to change the subject.

Amy uncurls her hand and holds out a letter. "They said they were willing to let me go in order to give me a better life. But I don't want a life without them. That's not a better life."

"My parents did the same thing, Amy. I know it couldn't have been easy to say goodbye to us. Everyone at Heaventree had parents or guardians who did the same. They knew something was going to happen. They knew how bad it was about to get."

"But they didn't say it in the letter."

"No, they couldn't. They didn't want to squash our emotions so soon. They probably knew that we'd all find out soon enough."

Amy goes quiet for a moment. Then she says, "My parents wrote something strange at the end, and I don't understand it." Amy brings the letter up to read it. "'We will always fight for the family.' If they sent me here, then they didn't fight for our family; they broke it apart."

Flare takes the letter in her own hands and reads the words to herself. We will always fight for the Family. The 'f' in Family is capitalized. She scans the rest of the letter. It's the only place they capitalized a word that wasn't a name. "I—I'm sure it just means they will keep praying for you, even if you guys are apart."

Flare hands Amy the letter again and stands up. Her mind is racing. She feels like she's on the verge of something, but she's not sure what. "Listen, I came up here to see if we can gather all the girls in our House. We need to get any and all creative types to begin working on the thing they do best. For me, it's drawing."

"Well, I play the flute," she says. "But why? What's that going to do?"

"I don't understand it all," says Flare, "but Miss Carmine left in her notes that the arts can be a form of worship. Creative praise somehow gives us access to God through the Holy Spirit. I don't understand it all yet, but...do you think you can help me get everyone together to, well, use their creative gifts? It's important."

Amy stands and walks to her desk. She tucks the letter back into it and reaches deep inside the drawer. She pulls out a silver flute and sticks it under her arm like a bayonet. "We don't have to understand, I guess."

Amy and Flare walk out of their room to enlist the others in their new assignment, though Flare can't shake her queasy stomach. It's dark now, and she wonders where her little brother is. It was her job to protect him. Always has been. But now...now she feels completely out of control. God only knows where Cornelius, Marcus and Atlys are. She has to leave it all in God's hands and pray He will protect them.

~ 7 ~

The skies outside of Heaventree are murky with clouds covering the moon. The landscape is desolate and empty like a ghost town. Old buildings and houses stand still and dark—spectors watching in the night.

"Are you sure this is the way back?" asks Atlys, holding the black dog close and tight on his leash.

"Yeah," says Cornelius. "We can't go back the way we came. Not with animals. It's too narrow. Mr. Deal said it's around here somewhere. Be on the lookout for some sign."

"What kind of sign?" asks Marcus.

"I don't know." Saying it out loud makes Cornelius feel like he might implode. He is leading two people and two dogs through dangerous territory and doesn't quite know what he's looking for.

They are on the other side of town now and crossing some railroad tracks. In the dark, they fumble and shine small flashlights a few feet in front of them.

"We should have figured this out when it was still light," says Atlys.

And she's right. How could he be so stupid? Cornelius

wonders. Of course, they should have planned their exit before they loaded up with any pets. His breathing grows heavy, and he can't speak.

Finally, they come to a small defunct gas station. There are no lights on inside and pumps that haven't been used in years. At the left of the peeling building, a tree stump sits to the side of the restroom door. Two rocks are stacked precariously on top.

"Look," says Cornelius. "I think that's it."

Quietly, the three creep over and assess the rocks. "Definitely manmade," says Atlys.

Cornelius looks around them and then motions for everyone to be quiet. He slowly turns the doorknob and opens the creaky door.

"You're not actually going to go in there, are you?" asks Atlys. "It's disgusting."

"Shhhh," says Cornelius as he enters the dark bathroom. The little Jack Russell Terrier he carries in his arm sniffs loudly.

"Two stones. And we're in a dirty place in the outskirts of town. What verse would this be?" Marcus asks Cornelius.

Cornelius closes his eyes a minute and then says, "Come in. Quick. And close the door." When all are in the tiny room safely, the odor becomes too much.

Atlys shines her flashlight on the old toilet, sink and hand dryer. A broken mirror shows the group's reflection in shards. Atlys straightens her red glasses and smoothes the top of her blonde hair.

"Leviticus 14:39-40," says Cornelius. "And the priest

shall come again on the seventh day, and look. If the disease has spread in the walls of the house, then the priest shall command that they take out the stones in which is the disease and throw them into an unclean place outside the city."

"This is definitely an unclean place outside the city," says Atlys.

"Look!" says Marcus.

The broken mirror is moving, reflective pieces fitting back in place. All of a sudden, it disappears altogether.

Cornelius shines his light there. "It's a passageway. Come on!"

Marcus climbs in first, and Cornelius hands him Roger the dog. Then Cornelius climbs through, and Atlys struggles to lift the black dog. "Here boy," coaxes Cornelius. He clicks his tongue, and the dog lifts up on its hind legs, putting its paws on the ledge where the mirror used to be. Atlys hands Cornelius the leash. He tugs a little, and the dog jumps through the opening. When Atlys is through as well, the opening disappears, and there is nothing there but a rocky wall.

"We made it," says Cornelius, breathing a sigh of relief. "There. Look over there. Tracks. The coal carts must be close by."

The group walks the tracks for a short while and then finds the carts waiting as promised.

"Okay, guys, it's time," says Atlys. She reaches into her backpack and pulls out a syringe and vial. "Here you go, boys. This will let you sleep on the ride. You'll be okay." After injecting them, she puts Roger into a small crate and ties the black dog's leash inside a cart, the three of them laying him down gently on the bottom.

Within a minute, both dogs are sound asleep. Cornelius utters the words that start the carts moving, and the three teens watch as the dogs head safely to Heaventree.

"Raymond is going to be so happy to see Roger again," he says, instantly left there with a mix of feelings—sadness because he'll never get to see his own dog Pepper again, and satisfaction knowing they just saved two animals from the devious plans of the Global Union. He also wishes he was headed back to Heaventree too. He misses Flare and the other kids. Misses Mr. Deal. But then he thinks of the celebration that will happen soon when the dogs arrive, and Heaventree knows that their mission has been successful.

So far.

"Come on," he says. "Let's rest here for a couple hours before heading back out again." The three teens sit against the wall on the side of the tracks. Cornelius pulls out some bread and peanut butter from his backpack, and they eat in silence and near darkness until he turns out his flashlight and rests his head on his pack. Feeling safe and hidden for the first time all day, within moments the three are fast asleep.

~ 8 ~

Flare and Amy are eating breakfast with their housemates, all twenty-four of them at a long table in the Main Hall. They've established that a group of creatives is forming a worship arts team that will meet every day. Flare and Sarah will do visual arts, Amy will play flute, Gina, Erin and Madeline will play guitar, piano and violin, and Banks will do creative writing. There's a certain excitement welling up in Flare, an eager anticipation of their creative minds all coming together. She's about to take another bite of her breakfast burrito when Josh Dunwright comes barrelling in the door.

"They made it! They brought some dogs back!"

"They're here? Corn is here?" asks Flare, standing up.

"They're not, no, but they sent two dogs here. You gotta see! They did it!"

The whole room empties. The teens all leave their plates and drinks unfinished on the tables and run out toward the Heaventree entrance. When they get there, Mr. Deal and Coach Arnold are walking toward them with the two dogs sent from the outside. Coach Arnold carries a small dog crate, and Mr. Deal walks with a black dog at his side, tail wagging.

"Whose are they?" asks Flare. "Do we know whose pets these are?"

"Well, let's find out," says Mr. Deal. "Looks like the whole campus is here." He leads them to the six house structures the students built, and everyone gives them a little space.

Mr. Deal leans down to the black dog and pets his head. He kneels down and whispers something.

Coach Arnold stops beside him and sets the crate down. He goes to open it and carefully pulls out a little shaking white dog.

"Roger!" A boy runs over to the dog and reaches for him. The little dog squirms to be free of Coach Arnold's arms and jumps down. He nearly tackles the boy, and the two hug and carry on until there isn't a dry eye around.

But the black dog still sits next to Mr. Deal, tail wagging and tongue sticking out.

"Does anyone know who this dog is?" he asks. He pets the dog's ears again and then pulls him close in a protective way. "You recognize anyone, dog?"

The dog turns and looks at him, then licks his face.

"Looks like he's yours," says Coach Arnold.

Mr. Deal stands up straight and brushes himself off.

"Well, I, we don't have time for pets around here. We have work to do. Josh, Raymond, you boys get these dogs situated in your house. There should be food and water, and it's your job to begin feeding them and walking them regularly. You understand?"

"Yes, sir," says Josh.

Raymond holds his little dog Roger and talks to him as he carries him into the house.

"And get going on those fences like we spoke about earlier. Each house will need an ample fence behind it for whatever animals make their way here. We can't have Heaventree crawling with creatures."

"Not a dog person?" asks Flare, teasing him.

"I, well, no, I've never had a pet."

"Never had a pet?" she says. "That's so sad."

"It just, I never...well, I don't know much—"

"They're not hard, they're worth it. You'll see."

"Well, if I were calling the shots, I wouldn't have ordered that we fill this beautiful campus with animals, but apparently God has other plans. I'm just following orders."

"And Cornelius did good," Flare says, beaming. "Now we know they can survive out there and get their job done."

She can't think of anything better than that. She has real hope that Cornelius is okay. Really okay. But she watches Raymond and wonders about his little dog. Where were his parents? Did they leave their dog behind?

Flare feels the sudden urge to see what's new in the Book of Martyrs, and she quietly leaves the bustling group of students to make her way to Castlebank. But someone's watching her leave the others. Flare doesn't know it, but she's being followed.

Flare's mind is swimming. Thoughts are coming at her from all angles, all at once. As she ducks behind the bushes and begins to press the Castlebank window open, she's thinking of Cornelius. What did he have to do in order to get those dogs to safety? She's almost envious, thinking of the excitement he must be seeing, but then she's equally fearful. Cornelius should be here. With her. Breaking into Castlebank.

Flare throws her leg up and over the sill and slips inside quietly. As she turns to shut the window, she nearly screams at the face staring back at her.

Eyes wide, she whispers, "Joe! What are you doing? You scared me to death!"

"Open up," he says. "I'm coming in too."

Taking a deep breath, Flare realizes she has no choice but to let him in. She puts her finger to her mouth to keep him quiet and then creeps through the room, stopping at the doorway to be sure the coast is clear. Flare and Joe make it to the door flanked with the stained glass windows of Genesis and Revelation on either side. "I am the Alpha and the Omega, the First and the Last, the Beginning and the End," says Flare. The door opens and Joe can't help but show his amazement.

"Shhh," says Flare as she watches Joe looking around the room. She remembers the first time she came in here. She was alone then and had no idea what she was going to find. Could never have dreamed it. Now, she goes to the middle of the room where a huge old book rests open. Joe was there the night she told Cornelius about a magic book that writes itself in Castlebank, but Joe has no idea that this is the Book of Martyrs. Flare silently prays that she doesn't see Joe's parents' names in here nor her parents'. She kneels and gets very still.

The pages before her are filled with names, new ones that weren't here the last time. Several dated today. She skims them to see if she recognizes anyone, but she doesn't. Flare realizes she's holding her breath and finally lets it out.

And then the page turns. On its own.

Joe backs up a few inches, stunned. He and Flare look at eachother. She knows there's someone else in the room with them, someone they can't see. An angel?

But Joe's mind is blown, and he's beginning to breathe heavily. Suddenly, the unmistakable scratching noise of pen on parchment begins, and they watch as black letters begin to form in cursive on the page.

Guerry Abraham Miser 3 September, Year of our Lord 2116

Miser. Miser. Flare wracks her brain but doesn't know the name. Still, she says a silent prayer for this man. *Please, Lord, bring him into your fold. Bring this soul home to Heaven with you in peace.*

Then she flips backward through the pages, scouring them for anyone she might know. She stops when she sees one.

Milo Spruil Abdul 3 September, Year of our Lord 2116

She points to the name, and Joe's face scrunches up. "Milo's Deli and Dry Cleaning?" he asks.

She nods.

"But what does it mean?"

Flare puts her finger to her mouth and grabs Joe's arm.

It's time to go. She'll tell him everything on the way back to Chizoba Hall. In a way, she feels comforted that she can share what she knows about the book with someone else. It's a hard burden to bear, having knowledge of who's still alive and who has succumbed to the war beyond Heaventree. But Milo was a real presence in their little community. His death hits so close to home. Too close.

~ 9 ~

Cornelius holds Atlys' elbow as they slip through the narrow crevice back onto Journey Street. He didn't mean to grab it—it was more of a reflex, but now that he's done it, his hands begin to sweat more than normal. He lets go and hopes she didn't notice. Behind him, Marcus whispers, "Almost there. Keeeeep going."

It's daybreak and birds are singing. Businesses aren't open yet, and no one is out on the streets. The teens stand on the sidewalk to get their bearings and catch their breath, Cornelius mostly. His claustrophobia wasn't quite so bad this time. That's progress.

He stops and looks across the street. The sign for Milo's Deli and Dry Cleaning is broken. It simply reads Milo's Del.

"Look," says Cornelius. He motions across the street.

"Windows are broken," says Marcus.

"Should we take a look?" asks Cornelius.

"What?" says Atlys. "No! Let's get going."

Pssst.

The three get still.

Pssst.

"Did you hear something?" asks Cornelius.

Pssst. Pssst.

He turns around and looks toward the bookstore behind him, Leaf. He walks closer and hears the door latch click. Instinctively, he backs up a step.

"Quick! In here!" a voice whispers. Cornelius is frozen. Should they run?

"Hurry, before someone sees you! It's okay. Please."

Something in the person's voice makes Cornelius open the door. "Come on!" he tells Atlys and Marcus, and the three walk into the dark bookstore, hearts in their throats.

Phhhht.

A match is struck, and a little light forms in front of a man. He's small and wearing an old apron. Walls of books flank the room, and stacks of them sit precariously on a desk. The man sets a candle there and the glow grows larger.

"I know who you are," says the man in a tinny voice with a strong accent.

The three teens stand perfectly still, muscles tensing, ready to run.

"It's too dangerous for you to be out there now."

"Don't I know you?" asks Cornelius.

"Michael Chang. I was a friend of Milo. This is my store."

"Yes, I've seen you. My parents...we used to buy books from here. What happened to Milo?" asks Cornelius.

"First they destroyed his business. Then they captured him. Killed him in the street."

"But why?"

Michael shakes his head and grabs a book off the desk.

He pulls it to him and sticks it in his apron pocket. "He couldn't stay quiet. I told him...Milo, you must not speak up now. It's too dangerous. Just as I am telling you now. They will get you. It will not be a GU solder with a gun, it will be a neighbor, someone you thought you knew."

"Why are you talking to us? You said you know who we are. Did you mean me, because my family shopped here?"

"You are from the school. I know of it. I have a nephew there. Evan Chang."

"Evan?" asks Cornelius. He turns and looks at Marcus. "He's in my house."

Marcus steps forward, standing at least a foot above this man. "Mr. Chang, why are you still here? Why haven't they come after you? Unless...you have the mark."

"No mark. No! I do not have it."

"So answer his question," says Atlys, crossing her arms.

The man grabs the candle and turns, walking toward a back room. "Follow me."

Cornelius begins to walk, but Atlys grabs his arm. "Wait! What if it's a trap!?"

"No trap. I promise," says Michael Chang. "Please, come."

Cornelius motions for Marcus and Atlys to stay where they are, and he follows the man through a narrow doorway covered with hanging colored scarves. The man turns on a light and the room is illuminated. It's long—much longer than he would have imagined—and filled with rows and rows of bookshelves. A musty odor hangs thick in the air.

"These books are very, very old," says Mr. Chang. "I have the most ancient books in the world. Here. I will show you."

The man walks to a shelf and carefully pulls out a large bound book. He carries it to a table and sets it down gently. Then he reaches in his apron and pulls out two white gloves and puts them on. Slowly, he opens the book and begins to show page by page of immaculate handwriting and drawings, colorfully painted in red, gold and blue. "This is the Book of Kells. Written over 1,300 years ago." He puts it back and goes to grab another. "This is The Codex Leicester, the scientific notebook of Leonardo da Vinci, over 600 years old."

"Mr. Chang, I don't want to be rude, but why are you showing me these books?"

Mr. Chang closes the book cover and quietly studies Cornelius' face. Slowly he says, "I have something for you. Something for you to take back to your school. You must give it to Mr. Deal. You must not let anyone else see it."

Cornelius looks back toward the colored scarves in the doorway. He wishes Marcus and Atlys were with him now. But they're not.

"You want me to take a book and not open it?"

"That is correct."

"May I ask why?"

Mr. Chang walks away from Cornelius and hurries down a long aisle. He is gone for more than a minute when he comes back holding a book in his glove-covered hands. "From all over the world, books come to me. Some I seek out. Others, they make their way by benefactors or serendipity." He sets the book down on a table and begins to wrap it in a thick cloth. "This one, here, is a book that few mortals have looked upon. It is a book that was given to me by those in another realm. It was spoken and written down. Then it was sealed. The seal has never been broken, and it must remain unbroken until..."

Mr. Chang finishes wrapping the cloth tightly with knotted twine.

"Until what?" asks Cornelius, his chest beginning to heave.

Mr. Chang looks at Cornelius, glancing from one eye to the other. "The seal may only be broken at the correct time and by the correct one."

"Is Mr. Deal the one to break it?"

Atlys peeks her head in the doorway and says, "Cornelius, it's late. We've got to get going!"

Mr. Chang puts the book in Cornelius' hands. "Hide this. Put it away and do not show the others. You must promise me."

Cornelius hoists his backpack, heavier now, onto his back and follows his friends to the door. He turns around to speak to Mr. Chang, but he's gone now. Mind racing, Cornelius stands at the door and listens, ear pressed up against it.

"We're going to have to be fast and keep our heads down. The street is busy now." He pulls his cap way down over his long bangs and prays they won't be noticed. Then he opens the door and squints in the sunlight. Time to focus again on the mission at hand. They've got to save more pets left behind. And now with a secret sealed book on his back, they've got even more reason to get back to Heaventree. Unharmed.

~ 10 ~

"Good morning, Heaventree!" Mr. Deal's voice comes over the loudspeaker. "It's time to rise and shine to our Great Purpose. God has plans for us today, but we each need to fortify before we get underway. The Main Hall is now open. Seeeee yaaa!"

Flare groans and rolls over, pulling her pillow over her head. She's exhausted. Why can't she sleep just a little longer?

Whap!

"Ow!" Flare pulls the pillow off of her head and expects to see her brother standing there, hitting her like he used to at home. But it's only Joe and Amy.

"You missed breakfast," says Amy. "And that was Joe, by the way."

"I...what? What time is it?"

"Almost ten. Are you feeling okay?"

Flare sits up. She didn't mean to fall back to sleep again. She rubs her eyes.

"I brought you food," says Amy, setting something wrapped in a napkin on her desk. "A cinnamon roll. But you better get ready quick. We're meeting the other creatives soon. Remember?"

"Gosh, yeah, I—give me a few minutes." She looks at Joe. "Can I have a little privacy, please?"

"Yeah," says Joe. "I gotta go anyway. For some reason I've been put on construction duty. I don't know why. I wasn't that good at it."

"None of us were," says Amy.

"Maybe that's all they think you can do," says Flare, standing and stretching. She grabs her pillow and throws it back at Joe.

"Missed me," he says, grinning and moving out the way. Then he heads out the door and closes it behind him.

Flare goes to brush her teeth. In the mirror, she sees Amy sitting down on the bed and staring out the window. Flare spits and turns around. "You all right?"

"Yeah, I'm just...missing my parents. And kind of missing Cornelius. Not missing, but I mean, wondering what's going on with him. With them. Know what I mean?"

Flare takes an extra long time washing her face and then dries it with a towel. "Yeah, I miss him, too. And I feel so helpless." Flare turns around and straightens up. "I'm sure he's fine though. They saved those dogs, right? I mean, it sounds as if they know what they're doing."

"I guess, but...well, nevermind."

"What?" asks Flare.

Amy begins to tear up a little. "What if they get caught?"

Flare walks to her desk and picks up her sketchbook and pencils. She grabs the wrapped cinnamon roll and shoves it on top, then starts walking to the door. "We can't think about that. They can't get caught. And besides, there's only one thing we can do to help."

"Right," says Amy. She reaches in her dresser drawer and grabs her flute. Then the two girls head out, already in silent prayer for the three teens risking their lives beyond Heaventree to fulfill their mission. The least they can do is fulfill theirs.

Meeting in the Conundra was Flare's idea. She wanted someplace with no distractions so the art created could be as pure as possible. The Conundra was built in the style of a traditional Japanese tea room with bare floors, rice paper walls and a simplicity and harmony unmatched on campus. The girls are waiting for her in the garden. It's an extension of the building, not just a place in front of it. Every plant, rock, path, bench and sculpture seems placed just so, as if it was always meant to be there.

"I love this place," says Gina, her guitar slung over her back.

"Me too," says Erin. She pulls up her violin and draws the bow slowly across the strings, creating an otherworldly hum to match the vibe of the garden.

"You guys want to stay in the garden and play your music while Sarah and I go inside for art?" asks Flare.

"Go on," says Amy, finding a bench to sit on near a graceful bonsai tree.

"What about you, Banks?"

Banks pulls her notebook to her chest and looks around. "I...think I'll stay out in the garden. Might write a poem about it."

"Okay, well, let's pray first," says Flare. The girls bow their heads. "Heavenly Father, we come here now to worship you alone. Please use our gifts for your glory. Fill us with your Holy Spirit and give us the notes to play, the words to write and the images to create. You are our Creator, and we are grateful to give our gifts back to you. Please watch over our friends and family on the outside of these walls. Protect them and bring us all together again soon. In Jesus' name we pray. Amen."

Inside the building are two rooms separated by a latticed wall of wood and paper. Flare can see the silhouette of Sarah in the other room. She can see her easel now set up and Sarah hunched over, mixing colors to paint.

Flare turns away and situates herself on the floor, back against an outer wall and knees up to support her sketchbook. She's working in charcoal today. She thinks back to the drawing she did before—the one with Cornelius, Marcus and Atlys—but she shoves the thought away. It was disturbing, and right now she needs to clear her mind of any worry, any cares, any thoughts at all.

Flare takes a deep breath and hears sweet music begin to play just outside. It's soft and sad, the violin seeming to weep in a duet with Amy's flute, then the guitar begins to play in harmony. Finally, the keyboard begins. How do they all play together so well? Flare wonders. She is swept away with the melody, and sits there for a while, just listening. When she opens her eyes, she no longer hears music, no longer sees her charcoal in hand or the paper. Flare sees a vision and she begins to sketch it, slowly at first, then quicker. She has no idea how much time is passing, but when she becomes alert, it's to the sound of Amy's voice. She looks up and realizes all the girls are standing over her. The music has stopped.

Amy kneels to the floor beside her. "You good?" she asks.

Flare takes a deep breath. "Yeah, good. Tired."

Amy takes the sketchbook from Flare's hands, stands and walks over to look at it in the sunlight coming through the doorway.

"You have black stuff all over you. All over your hands and face," says Gina.

"Here," says Sarah, handing Flare a rag that smells like dried paint. Flare wipes her face and looks over to Amy, who is now back outside, sitting beside her flute.

Flare goes to her and asks, "What is it? What did I draw?"

"You don't know?" asks Amy.

"I never know. Never aware of it. It's like...someone else takes over."

Flare sits beside her and looks down at the drawing. It's a house, strong and lovely on one side with a garden and picket fence. But the other side is crumbled and smoldering as if burned from a fire or a bomb.

"What in the world?" asks Flare. "How could my art, I mean, something I did in prayer and worship, turn out so dark?" She takes the sketchbook from Amy's hands.

"I know," says Amy.

"You can't know. Your music was so beautiful; it was sweet and lovely—"

"I mean I know because I know this house." Amy

looks at Flare and then down at the drawing. "It's my house," she says. "That's my bedroom. That's the mango tree we planted three years ago. That's the little stained glass window in the kitchen. It's my house, Flare! And it's destroyed."

Flare feels her blood rush out of her. How could she have this vision? Why did she have to draw this? She wasn't ready to tell Amy about her parents! Tears fill her eyes and spill over. Before she knows it, she is holding her friend tight and sobbing. "I should have told you," Flare says. "Please forgive me."

"Forgive you what?" asks Amy, backing up.

Flare wipes her face, smeared in black now. "There's something I should have told you a few days ago, but I didn't know how. I didn't...want to hurt you."

"Tell me. Please, now," says Amy, her voice low and even.

So Flare takes a deep breath and shares what she knows about the Book of Martyrs. And how she saw Amy's parents listed in it. When she's done, all the girls are bent around Amy, holding her as her face contorts and she screams without a sound.

~ 11 ~

Flare and Amy have been sitting silently by the lake for a while now. Flare just wants to be there for her, to listen if she wants to talk. She can't imagine what it feels like to lose her parents. Doesn't want to imagine it.

The blare of a horn signals a new arrival from outside of Heaventree.

"Animals," says Flare, getting up quickly. "They sent some pets. Let's go see." Flare grabs Amy's arm and hoists her up. They both begin to jog, eager to see what Cornelius, Marcus and Atlys have done.

A large group of teens forms near the entrance of Heaventree. Flare watches anxiously. She grabs Amy's hand and squeezes it.

Finally, Josh, Raymond, Mr. Deal and Coach Arnold arrive with not just one or two dogs, but five dogs. Josh is also carrying two small kennels that move, sway and squirm. He sets them down and Flare runs over.

"Cats!" she says. "And look! Kittens!"

The crowd is loud and excited, but Mr. Deal quiets everyone down. "There's a note," he says. "Names of these pet owners. If I call your name, kindly come claim your pet and get him or her—or it—situated in your house. Right-O. Here goes."

As the names are called, teens squeal and run to grab friends. The dogs are overjoyed to be reunited with their owners, but the cats, well, they seem as if they couldn't care less. There is so much happiness in this moment, Flare almost forgets the deep sadness Amy is experiencing. Almost, but not quite.

Joe comes to them covered in sawdust. "Hey, that was pretty awesome. Cornelius is rocking it out there. It's great, huh?"

"Yeah, it is."

Joe looks from Flare to Amy and back again. "What—what's going on? Something wrong?"

Flare glares at Joe and mouths something to him. She's trying to get him to shut up.

"It's my parents," says Amy quietly. "They're...dead."

"What? What are you talking about?" Joe fumbles. "Oh no, that's—"

"The Book of Martyrs," Flare says. "They were in it."

"You know about the book too?" asks Amy, a bit defensive.

"Yeah," says Joe. "I—well, I followed Flare and—"

"He didn't know about your parents," says Flare. "He only saw the book once and just for a minute."

"So everybody knew about it but me," she says.

Flare is at a loss for words.

"I want to see it," says Amy, resolutely. "I want to see with my own eyes. And if people's family members are dying out there and Heaventree has a way of knowing who's dying, then they ought to let us know."

Amy looks up and watches Mr. Deal walking beside Coach Arnold back toward campus. She firms up and marches over to him.

Flare and Joe watch in horror. Amy is such a sweet, mild-mannered girl, but at this moment, Mr. Deal has come under her wrath. Her hands are flying in the air, and her voice is raised. Mr. Deal looks squarely at Flare and crosses his arms. Finally, the three of them, Amy, Mr. Deal and Coach Arnold begin walking toward Castlebank, Coach Arnold's arm around Amy's shoulders.

Flare can't let Amy go there without a friend at her side. She and Joe run over and join them. Not a sound is heard but the stomping of feet and heavy breathing from all. Flare bites her lip and falls into line. She can almost feel the tension, like a thick black cloud hovering above. At any moment, lightning might strike.

~ 12 ~

"It's not enough." Atlys crosses her arms and stops to watch the coal cars carrying three cats, two dogs and a pair of birds in a cage off to Heaventree.

"What do you mean?" asks Marcus. He leans against the wall and slides down, exhausted. Several days on the run, sneaking into houses, taking animals to safety, all while trying not to be seen, is beginning to take its toll on the three teens.

Cornelius is already on the floor and reaches up to hand Marcus an apple.

"It's not enough!" Atlys says. "This! Taking animals back to safety. What about the people out there who we know are in hiding? What about our parents, our families and friends? Why aren't we trying to save them instead?"

"That's not the mission," says Cornelius, matter-of-fact-like. "Our mission is to save the animals."

The sound of the carts rolling in the distance fills the tunnel. Marcus takes a bite of his apple and says, "It's not for us to understand, but to obey what we've been told to do. Everything in God's timing."

Atlys lets her arms down and lowers herself next to the

boys on the wall. She puts her hand out to Cornelius, who hands her an apple as well.

"I know it's hard," he says, "thinking about the people out there who must be hiding, but we have to believe they're okay. I have to believe it. And I have to believe that every pet we rescue isn't just saving the animal's life, it's saving the owner's life. If the pet is safe, the GU can't use it against them and track down the owner."

"I know that," says Atlys, "I do. I just..." Atlys puts her hands to her face and tries to hold back tears. Cornelius instinctively puts his hand on her shoulder.

"S'okay," he says.

Marcus is quiet for a moment. Then he says, "I miss my family. Every home we enter reminds me of a family torn apart. I think of my mother, smiling at me, and I miss her face, her voice. I just..."

The three teens are completely quiet. After a while, the sound of crunching apples can be heard, but then nothing as Cornelius, Atlys and Marcus allow their minds to travel to their loved ones, wondering if they're okay, praying they are, praying for the strength to go another day on their mission. It's important; they know that. But it's wearing them down slowly like water running over limestone. Cornelius falls asleep in the middle of a prayer, asking God to protect them from the evil one.

And they sleep in still, dark sadness while the flashlight acts as watchman, casting light and shadows on the other side of the tunnel.

The tunnel is strange. In the beginning, Cornelius

knew what to expect when he walked through the door. It opened to the old Heaventree campus which led to Journey Street, Leaf Bookstore and so on. But now, each time they wake up and leave the tunnel, they enter a new place, a new city or town. It's a little disconcerting. Marcus likened it to riding on a train, each stop taking them someplace new.

The three teens rub their eyes and try to adjust to the daylight. This town looks nothing like where they've been before. It's a bustling city, with cars whizzing by and highrises. People are everywhere, walking along the sidewalks, heading here, heading there. The three are alarmed and pull their hats down lower on their heads.

"This way," says Cornelius. "Keep walking and don't call attention to yourselves." They walk quickly, getting in line with a group of sidewalkers, heading to what looks like a subway station. When they get closer, they realize where they are.

"Metrovia," says Marcus under his breath.

"We need to check the map," says Cornelius. He looks all around. Nowhere seems to be private.

"In here," says Atlys. She darts to the right and down a long dirty alleyway between two buildings. They hide behind a smelly dumpster, kneel on the ground and unfold the map.

"There are three kids from this city," says Cornelius. "One in an apartment building and two others on the outskirts of town. Looks like they were neighbors."

"Shh. Do you hear that?" whispers Atlys. The three get completely still and hold their breaths. Suddenly a cat jumps out of the trash and hisses at them. It grabs a spoiled piece of meat in its mouth and scurries down the alley.

"Scared me to death!" says Cornelius, breathing heavy and trying to laugh.

But their adrenaline is pumping now. They have to navigate a foreign city full of GUYs without being seen. Cornelius knows they've done it several times before, but somehow, it isn't getting easier. And with each passing day, the animals left behind are getting hungrier and weaker. They've already found two pets dead in their homes. The thought of it drives a sense of urgency in Cornelius.

He points to the map and says, "We're three blocks away from this building. But the apartment is pretty high up. We can't afford to take the elevator, so we'll need to find the stairs."

"It's a mastiff, Cornelius," says Atlys. "How in the world are we going to walk through the city with a dog that huge without calling attention to ourselves?"

"Come on, let's go," says Cornelius. But his mind is whirring, searching the Scriptures, praying for an answer to her question.

When they reach the brick building, they walk around the side for the stairs exit. Up and up and up they go to the eighth floor. "Who keeps a mastiff in an apartment, anyway?" asks Atlys. It's a rhetorical question. They've each had the same thought.

At the door of apartment 8C, they stop and assess the situation. It's a metal door. The door is locked. This is the only way in.

Marcus peers in the peephole. "Nothing," he says.

"Can't you do what you did at that place in Belshire?" says Cornelius. "Just pick the lock."

"Easier said than done. But...here goes."

Marcus opens his bag and pulls out a tool. He puts his ear to the door and jiggles the knob. "If only my mother could see me now. She'd be so proud," he says.

As he continues to work, Cornelius looks down the long hall, praying no one comes. He and Atlys cover Marcus from view. And then they hear a strange noise. A loud sniffing. Cornelius walks a few steps toward it. The sniffing gets louder. Then scratching.

"Are you sure this is the apartment, Cornelius?" asks Marcus.

"You saw it just like I did."

Cornelius gets close to the door marked 8F. He stops in front of it and leans down to the ground. He puts his hand to the door. The sniffing picks up. Cornelius looks through the peephole and says quietly, "I think we found our dog, guys. Unless there's another mastiff on this floor."

He carefully turns the knob and...it clicks open. Cornelius can hear the t.v. in another room. He hears dishes clinking and water running from the kitchen. When he pushes the door open a few inches, a large nose sticks out and sniffs him.

"Wally?" he says. "That you, boy?" The huge dog wags its tail.

"Atlys, quick!" says Cornelius. She darts forward and in a few seconds, the great beast is leashed and the group is back in the stairwell. When they know they are alone, she gives him a handful of dog food, which he gobbles up.

"He's starving," she says. "And look how he sits. He's weak. I hope he can get through the city." Atlys reaches in her bag and pulls out a syringe. "Here you go, Wally. This will help you feel better. This is a high dose of Vitamin B."

She follows it up with a bottle of water, which he slurps.

"Quick," says Cornelius. "If they find him gone, they'll come after him." So the teens and the 200 pound dog move as quickly down the stairs as they can. The dog is panting by the time they reach the street.

As they walk along the sidewalk, trying to blend in with the crowd and not be seen, they take as many alleyways as they can. But at a street crossing, a little boy looks over and points at the dog. He pulls on his mother's arm. "Look at that, Mom! A mastiff! It weighs up to 200 pounds and is known to be loyal and drools excessively."

"That's nice," says the mother. "Nice dog," she says to Atlys. "Is he much trouble?"

"No, not really," says Atlys, her head dropping lower to keep the woman's gaze from her face. She leans down and pets the dog.

When the pedestrians begin to walk across the street, the three teens and Wally begin crossing as well. But then something goes terribly wrong.

Wally sits down. Right there in the middle of the road. Everyone is looking at him. Atlys is pulling on the leash and the boys are coaxing him. But the enormous dog won't move.

Cornelius can feel all eyes on them and panic begins to swell in his throat.

"What do we do?" asks Marcus, attempting to shove the dog's hind quarters.

Cornelius doesn't have time to think, but a verse is given to him. It rushes out of him like a breath. "Lord, strike this people with blindness."

Suddenly, chaos erupts. People scream and run into one another. A car crashes into another and a horn goes off. The people all around them are blinded, including the little boy and his mother. They grope the air and break into tears.

"Pick him up!" shouts Cornelius.

The three teens struggle to lift Wally's front and back legs, but between them, they have him up in the air long enough to get them to a more secluded spot in an alleyway behind another smelly dumpster.

"That was unbelievable!" says Marcus. "Never seen anything like it! I mean, you prayed to make those people blind!"

"Well, actually, I was only repeating a verse in the Bible. In Second Kings, the prophet Elisha says that prayer to escape the Syrians. He also asked the Lord to give supernatural sight to the young man with him, and when his eyes were opened, he saw the chariots and horses of heaven all around them. We have to remember that, you know. Even when we think we're in trouble, we're surrounded by God's armies."

The three are quiet for a moment, letting that sink in and looking all around them in wonder.

"Oh yeah," says Cornelius. "Lord, thank you for answering my prayer back there, but if you don't mind, please let all those people see again." He looks at Marcus. "You ready to get going?"

"He'll have to stay here a while," says Atlys. "I'll feed and water him until he's strong enough to walk again. You two will have to go on to the other houses alone."

"We can't split up," says Cornelius. "We made a promise to Mr. Deal."

"Yeah, well, Deal's not out here with us, is he? He doesn't know what we're facing here."

"Maybe she's right," says Marcus.

"No, says Cornelius. "I'm not leaving you. We stick together."

~ 13 ~

At the picnic tables behind the Main Hall, Flare, Josh and Nattie are meeting. "Each new successful mission brings them closer to getting caught," says Nattie about the other heads of the houses of Heaventree, Cornelius, Marcus and Atlys. "It's math. Statistics and probability."

"Then they'll beat the odds," says Flare, annoyed. "All things are possible with God, remember? Even things that are statistically improbable."

"I guess," says Nattie.

"She's right," says Josh, running his hands through his hair.

"Who's right?" asks Flare.

"You both are."

The three sit in silence, watching a flock of geese waddle up onto the bank of the lake. They were spooked out of the water because of the construction going on in the middle on the tiny island there.

"What are they doing?" asks Flare. "Joe and all those other kids. What in the world are they building in the middle of a lake?"

"Looks like a treehouse," says Josh. "My guess is they're going to build up around that big tree."

"But why didn't they ask you to help?" asks Nattie. "You were pretty great at construction."

"I don't know, and I don't care," says Josh. "I'm enjoying a break from all that hammering and lifting." He rubs his shoulder, and the girls turn away when they catch a glimpse of his flexed bicep.

"Yeah, well, I hope I get to go up in the treehouse when it's done," says Flare. "Corn and I had one in our backyard. We practically grew up in it."

"I had one too," says Josh.

"There were some kids across the street who had a treehouse," says Nattie. "It was really nice. They let me use it until...well, until they got their marks."

The three turn quiet, remembering their homes, their families, their childhoods. They watch as a little boat brings over more supplies and drops them at the island in the center of the lake.

Josh begins to stand up. "I've got to get back to the dogs," he says. "It's feeding time or walking time or bath time for somebody. You wouldn't believe how much attention these dogs need. Especially the black one that nobody claimed. He's kind of needy."

"Well, maybe he's your dog then," says Nattie. "Have you named him?"

"No," says Josh. "And I wouldn't say he's my dog. He's really into Mr. Deal. He sorta flips out every time he's near."

"So he's Deal's dog," says Flare.

"Not sure Deal sees it that way," says Josh. "Hey, you, uh, you wanna walk with me back to the house?"

Nattie and Flare look at Josh, a little stunned, flushed even, but it's apparent, he was looking at Flare.

"You—you guys go on," says Nattie. "I've got to...go do something I forgot."

"Oh, okay," says Flare, tucking a red lock of hair behind her ear. "See you later. I guess I'll go help with the animals."

Flare stands and her knees feel weak. And did it suddenly get really hot out here? She sees Josh walking a few steps ahead of her. Sees his broad shoulders and tanned legs and...she catches her breath, steels herself and then follows him, rushing to catch up.

"So this is the House of Josh," Flare teases, as they enter the house and a blur of dogs flies by.

"Mi casa," he says.

"Kinda smells in here, doesn't it?"

Josh reaches down and grabs a dog as it's running past him. "Whoa, whoa, Roger. Whew! Dude, you need a bath. And I've got just the person to do it," he says.

"What, me? No way," says Flare.

"Oh, come on. We'll be a good team. I'll wash and you dry. Unless you'd like to switch."

Flare couldn't say no to his dimples if she tried. What was happening to her? When they met ten days ago, she was strong and had her guard up against his good looks. But now, he was a nice guy, too, and nice, added to the looks, well, it was a recipe for disaster.

"I guess I'll dry," says Flare.

Josh carries Roger to a bathtub, fitted with a handheld shower head. He sets the little dog in the tub and then slowly turns the water on, feeling it with his hand until it's the right temperature. Then he runs the water gently over the dog who's shaking now.

"Aw, it's okay," says Flare.

"Can you grab me the shampoo?" asks Josh.

Flare goes to the counter and grabs the bottle, then kneels down beside Josh and pets Roger's wet head. She smiles at him. Her heart pounds. She's so close to Josh. Her mind is reeling.

"Look at you, little dude," says Josh. He lathers the dog and fashions bubbles on the top of his head. "You like your bubble hat?" he asks. "Well, it's time to get clean. Hold your breath."

Josh carefully holds his hand over the little dog's eyes while he rinses the soap from his head, his back, his tail and feet. When he shuts the water off, Roger looks like a wet rat. Josh squeezes the excess water from his fur. "Grab me a towel, would you?"

Flare gets up to go to the closet, but as soon as she does, Roger shakes as hard as he can, and Josh squeals. When Flare returns, Josh is wiping his soaking wet face. She takes the towel and touches it to his cheek. "Looks like you might need this more than Roger," she says, stifling a giggle.

Josh grins while he dries off, then rubs the towel on the little dog until he is shiny clean. "All right, Roger," Josh says. "Now, don't get dirty again. At least not for a while."

He picks up the dog and sets him on the floor. As soon as his paws hit wood, Roger tears out of the room like a wild animal, slipping and sliding around the corners.

"Well, that was fun," says Flare.

"For you, maybe," he says. "And I'm glad you thought it was fun. Because we have..." Josh pulls his hand up and starts counting his fingers. "Six more dogs left."

"And two cats with kittens," she says.

"I'm pretty sure the cats can handle themselves," he says. Josh stands up and turns to the door. "Time for the next one. You—you don't have to stay if you don't want to."

"Well, from the looks of that little dog, it seems you need all the help you can get."

Josh smiles at her and smooths his wet hair on his forehead. "Thanks," he says. "Be right back."

Flare watches the suds burst and run down the drain and realizes she feels...happy. It's a feeling she hasn't had since they left home. It rushes on her with no warning and is met with a mixture of guilt and dread. She doesn't know what her brother, Cornelius, is facing right this minute. But she feels connected to him, somehow, through the dogs he's rescued. When Josh enters the doorway carrying a big bulldog, she feels a lump in her throat for Josh and for her brother.

He's out there. Somewhere. She prays he's okay.

~ 14 ~

"Wally needs to get back to Heaventree now," says Atlys. "You guys both know I'm right. He needs medical attention and rest."

The huge mastiff lays his head on the ground and closes his eyes while Atlys pets him. Cornelius considers the options. They either let her wait here with the dog behind this dumpster until they get the other two...but how long will that be, really? Or they all go take Wally to Heaventree and then go back out for the others. Cornelius shudders as he remembers finding that golden retriever dead in his home. He doesn't want to see that again. Doesn't want any more animals to die. But he knows what he has to do.

"We won't separate. It's too dangerous," he says. "We'll take Wally back and then hurry to find the other two dogs. They're side by side, so it's just a matter of making it to the neighborhood."

"Then let's go," says Marcus. He leans down and rubs the dog's head. "You ready, old boy? Time to leave."

Marcus, Cornelius and Atlys hoist the dog up to standing and then begin moving back the way they came. If they stay in the alleyways and avoid the main streets, they should be able to make it unseen. But the walk is slower than Cornelius would like. When they finally make it to the portal, this time a ticket window in an abandoned movie theater, the dog is barely moving. Atlys gives him a drink and then they lift him up and over. Marcus comes in last, and the wall turns to rock again, closing them off from the outside world.

They've returned to the tunnels, and relief floods Cornelius. Wouldn't it be nice to just ride the coal car back with Wally and be done with this mission? Part of him—a big part—just wants to call it a day. How many days has it been on the run? They've rescued lots of pets already, right? Is that enough?

No. He knows it's not. Cornelius feels the weight of his backpack on his shoulders. The list of pets and their locations is heavy on his heart. And the secret sealed book from Mr. Chang is like a boulder around his neck. Keeping secrets from his friends seems the biggest burden to bear.

After Wally is safely in a coal car, moving toward Heaventree, the three teens turn around and take deep breaths. "Let's be on our way then," says Cornelius. He pulls a water bottle out of his bag and guzzles it.

"I'm exhausted," says Atlys. "And my feet hurt."

"We're all tired," says Marcus, "but we have no alternative but to carry on."

Cornelius doesn't want to mention that every muscle in his body aches, he's starving and would give his right ear for a hot shower. But this is no time to rest.

When Cornelius steps out of the portal this time, he

smells smoke. Everything is dusty, and the sun is covered up, creating a thick yellow haze. Instinctively, he pulls his shirt up over his nose to filter the air.

"What in the world?" asks Atlys.

"Destruction," says Marcus. "Maybe we're too late."

They walk along what was once a road, but now is just rock and asphalt ripped up and tossed about like pebbles. They move along silently, tripping now and again, until they reach what was an intersection.

"Which way?" whispers Marcus.

Cornelius holds the map close to his face and points to the left. "We take this road for another mile or so." He tucks the map safely away and presses gently on Atlys' back. "Sorry your feet hurt," he says. "Mine do too."

"I know," says Atlys. "But we're in this thing together."

"Together," says Marcus, turning around slightly. Just then, he falls back on Atlys and Cornelius, and they all hit the ground.

"What the—"

"You okay?" asks Cornelius, struggling to get upright.

"Yeah, I just..tripped, I guess," says Marcus.

"Then can you get off me?" asks Atlys. "I—oh, God, blood. I'm bleeding!"

Cornelius bends down and inspects. He breathes deeply. "It's not your blood, Atlys. Marcus? You okay, buddy?"

Marcus looks down and sees his left arm. There is blood running down it.

"You've been shot," says Cornelius. "Quick, we have to get off the road." He grabs his friend and hurries him to a blown out storefront. There are creepy mannequins strewn across the floor. Cornelius runs to one and pulls off a dress. He rips the fabric and wraps it around Marcus' arm.

"Here, let me do that," says Atlys. She pushes hard on the area and Marcus squirms.

They all hear something outside. The whistle and bang of gunshots. Here and off in the distance.

"So they know we're here," says Marcus, sweating now.

"Maybe," says Cornelius. He goes to the window and peers out. "Or maybe we only got caught in stray fire. It's too dusty out there for anyone to see us."

"Hey, well that is good news," says Marcus, trying to laugh.

"I'm going to give you something for the pain, Marcus," says Atlys. "Just enough to take the edge off. The bullet didn't even lodge in your skin. Looks like it just grazed you. If we can get this bleeding to stop, you'll be just fine."

Atlys pulls out a syringe and fills it halfway, then she gives the shot in Marcus' arm. He doesn't even flinch. After a few minutes and some fresh water, the three sit on the ground of the store and look at eachother.

"It's time to move," says Marcus.

"No," says Cornelius. "You just got shot! You've got to get back to Heaventree."

"It's not life-threatening, and anyway, we have come this far. I do not want to turn back now."

"Is it just the drugs talking?" Cornelius asks Atlys.

"No, I think he's right," she says. "Let's just go get these next two and then we'll reassess what to do from there."

"This goes against all of my better judgment," says

Cornelius. "One of us just got shot. Live fire's all around us. We're not equipped for this. I'm not trained for this."

The teens are quiet and thinking. Cornelius begins to pray. Finally he musters, "Well, if you guys are crazy enough to keep going, I guess...I am too. Come on."

~ 15 ~

Flare stares at the ceiling, waiting for Mr. Deal to come over the loudspeaker. She sticks her finger in the end of her cast and scratches an itch. Daylight is beginning to break. She thinks about how warm and comfortable she is in this bed, under her sheets, in a dry safe room. But what about Cornelius? Where is he sleeping? Does he sleep? Does he feel warmth and comfort, or is it dreadful every second?

She cannot believe how brave he is. Her opinion of her little brother has changed completely since they left home. He's much more capable than she ever imagined him to be. She considered herself the strong one. No longer.

Flare hears Amy turn over in her bed. She's been extremely quiet since she learned her parents were dead, and who could blame her? She's not the same. Maybe she never will be. Her soft edges have grown hard.

Since she learned about the Book of Martyrs, Amy has become obsessed with discovering who has been killed on the outside. But what will happen when she learns of someone's parents dying? Will she run and tell the kid?

She'll see how hard it is then. Do you shatter someone's hope just to get at the truth? Or is it more humane to hold the news until a better time?

But can there ever be a good time to learn that someone you love is gone?

Flare pulls the covers up over her head.

"Good morning, Heaventree!" says Mr. Deal over the speakers in the ceiling. "I hope the sound of my voice finds you well and awake and ready for the day ahead. What will it bring? God only knows. But He'll be with us in it...whatever comes our way. And hey, rumor has it the kitchen is serving the ever popular French toast, so better get a move on. Beeeeat ya there!"

Flare yawns and pushes to sitting, then she swings her legs over and onto the floor. Before she can stand up, Amy says, "I need to see the book."

Flare knows which book she's talking about, and it hurts her, knowing she will look again at the names of her deceased parents.

"I want to know how it happened," she says. "How did they die?"

"We'll probably never know, Amy. I'm so sorry. But..." She tried to choose her words carefully. "Isn't it more important how they lived? I mean, they truly lived. Didn't they? In Christ. And so should we." The room is completely silent for nearly a minute. Finally, Flare says, "Let's have our creative worship session this morning after breakfast. Like we planned. And then we can see the book again. Okay?"

Amy is pressing up and catches Flare's eye. She nods slightly, and Flare can finally take a breath again.

On the way to breakfast, it's obvious there's a commotion going on at the gate. The girls jog over with everyone else and press through a crowd of students to see the biggest dog they've ever witnessed.

"Wally," says a boy, bending down to read the dog tag. "His name is Wally. Anybody know who—"

"Wally!" shrieks a girl, no bigger than a mite. She barrels through and wraps herself around Wally's neck, burying her face in his fur and crying. Seeing it brings Flare to near tears herself. The fresh, raw emotion of missing loved ones is thick in the air. Everyone at Heaventree is feeling it.

"He did it again," says Amy.

Flare looks over at her friend. Amy's watching the sweet reunion with her hands over her mouth. Finally, she lets them down and the barest trace of a smile graces her lips. "Cornelius saved another one. That means...he's all right." Amy straightens her back and puts her arm around Flare. "Come on, let's go eat," she says, and Flare dutifully, gratefully follows.

At breakfast, Flare is enjoying way too much maple syrup, slopping the pieces of toast around on her plate, when Mr. Deal takes the seat next to her. He sips his coffee and taps the table as if announcing his presence.

"I'm thinking we send a little care package to the kids on the outside this morning," he says. "Something to boost their morale, maybe. Any ideas?"

"Brownies," says Amy, wiping her mouth with a napkin. "Or cookies."

Flare is pensive. This is her chance to communicate with her brother, to encourage him, to let him know she cares.

"Corn has this bear," she says. "This stupid stuffed bear. I guess, no, that wouldn't work."

"Although that is...very sweet, and very, ahem, sad...I think maybe brownies may be in order. Or first aid. And deodorant. I realize I sent them out there, but the thought of having no shower is, well..."

"How about clean clothes? Or clean sleeping bags?" says Amy.

Mr. Deal's eyes light up. "Now we're talking. All right. I'll get on it and get that package ready. If there's anything else you think they might need or want, let me know."

Mr. Deal makes a beeline for the door where, surprise, the black dog is waiting for him.

"Wow," says Flare. "Deal, can't go anywhere without that dog by his side."

"Maybe the dog sees another lonely soul in him."

"Maybe so." Flare stares into her syrup, the glare of the window shining in it. She moves her fork a little as a thought enters her mind. It flits around and then settles on her heart. Should she do it? She's conflicted. And anyway, the image she drew is no longer in her hands, it's with Professor Moss. But that doesn't mean she can't recreate it. She remembers what it looks like. Isn't this the one thing she can give her brother? Give them all? A warning about what's to come, or hopefully, what could come unless they change their plans?

Flare stands and pushes her chair back with her knees. "I—I have to go do something. I forgot. I'll meet you at the Conundra in twenty minutes."

"Okay, I guess I'll see you there."

Flare's pulse is racing, her hand scribbling as fast as she can. When the drawing is complete, she second-guesses herself for just a second, then folds it and stuffs it in an envelope, sealing it as she runs across campus to the Heaventree gate. She catches Mr. Deal walking with the black dog. He's holding a small pack. "Ah, Miss Flanagan, did you think of anything else to add?"

The black dog stops and startles, turning toward Flare and growling. "Dog, dog, be quiet, it's just Flare. I don't know what's going on with this dog. What is it with dogs? Do they just follow you around or what?"

"That's why people like them," says Flare. "They're loyal."

"Loyal, huh?" Mr. Deal looks at the dog who sneezes and sits, looking intently at his new master.

"I wanted Corn to have this. It's just a note. You know, encouraging him, Bible verses. Stuff like that."

"Okay, then put it in here. I'm running out there now. He should have it by this evening." Mr. Deal watches as Flare sets the envelope on top of a plate of brownies. He closes the pack and then says. "I do know how hard this is for you, knowing he's out there...I just...I realize your sacrifice, I mean, the worry you must be fighting. You're still his big sister."

"That's right," says Flare. "And I'll always protect him. The best way I can." Flare walks off, knowing she's done the right thing, sending him that drawing. Cornelius has to know the truth about Atlys...that she'll turn on them in time. That she'll succumb and become...the enemy.

~ 16 ~

The sounds of gunfire stopped a while ago. Marcus is fast asleep, holding his arm, leaning against the wall of the shop they landed in. Cornelius and Atlys stare off at the mannequins. They're so eerie. Finally, Atlys presses to standing and walks to the opposite wall. She's looking at the clothing, the shoes. She tries a pair on. "Hey, they fit!" she says. She rifles through the hangers and finds a shirt she likes. Carefully, she folds it tight and stuffs it in her pack.

"So we're stealing now?" asks Cornelius, sort of joking, but not completely.

"This store is destroyed," she says. "The owners are nowhere to be found. I would be stupid to pass up provisions when I find them. You guys ought to look around too."

"It wouldn't hurt to find some black clothing," says Cornelius. "It might make us harder to see."

"I'm already hard to see," says Marcus, piping up and stirring on the ground. He smiles at them.

"Hey, buddy, you doing okay?" asks Cornelius. "We thought you needed the rest. Has the bleeding stopped?"

Atlys comes to him and kneels down. She rips another

piece of cloth to replace the dressing. "Yep," she says. "It's looking pretty good. You feel like moving?"

"What time is it?" asks Marcus.

"After six. It'll be getting dark soon."

Cornelius pulls out his map and tries to identify where they are now and where they need to go. "It's seriously only about a mile away," she says. "See these two houses beside each other?"

All packed up and rested, the three teens head out carefully onto the sidewalk again. The dust has settled somewhat, and they can see the broken windows and burned out buildings across the street. The path they need to follow will take them further away from the storefronts.

They walk carefully and in silence for about ten minutes. Finally, the houses begin to dot the sides of the road and suddenly they're in a more suburban area. A neighborhood. The houses here are of modest size but cookie cutters. They all look the same. Some have the driveway on the right and others on the left, but that's the extent of the variety. Each has a little fenced in square yard of what used to be grass in the back. These houses don't look occupied for the most part. But what if they are? What it GUYs are living here now? Cornelius pulls his cap down lower on his forehead and makes sure his bangs come down over his eyebrows.

"Up there," he says. "The third one on the right. And the one after it. I think."

He hopes he's right. A wrong move on an occupied house could mean the worst for all of them.

When they approach the gray house, they notice the

shrubs are completely overgrown and covering the windows. Around back they find one that Marcus can open. It only lifts a few inches and then hits something hard.

"There's a piece of wood or something in the way," he mutters. He reaches his good arm in and tries to move it, to no avail. "Can't reach. My arm's too thick."

"I guess this is where my wimpiness finally comes into good use," says Cornelius. He switches places with Marcus and attempts the same. "Not...reaching..." he says, straining.

"Let me do it," says Atlys, but Cornelius won't quit trying. "Seriously, move it!"

Atlys positions her body differently than the boys did and after a minute is about to push the wood out of the way. The window releases all the way up. "And that is how it's done," she says, brushing off her hands and straightening her glasses. "After you."

The three crawl into the home, but they see no signs of a living animal. They scour each room a couple times, but nothing. Cornelius sits down on the sofa and lays his map out on the coffee table. "This is the right house. See? I know it."

"Maybe we should check the other house next door," says Marcus. "Maybe they are together, these dogs."

"I'll go," says Atlys.

"We'll all go," says Cornelius. His stomach is uneasy. It's been this way since the moment they left Heaventree. Part of him wants to stay right here in this house. If he could only take a nap in a real bed. Or shower. Or...

"Er, you two, you go ahead. I just need to do something for a minute." He eyes the bathroom. How long has it been since he used a real toilet? With real toilet paper?"

"We can wait for you," says Marcus, smirking. "How long will you be?"

"Not long, but...you go ahead. I'll catch up with you. It—it's just next door. It's not like we're really separating."

Honestly, Cornelius doesn't know how long his "business" will take. He ushers them out and shuts the bathroom door.

As he sits there, he thinks back to their week of adventure. He remembers each and every animal they rescued along with the houses they entered. He tries to imagine the reunions of people and pets back at Heaventree. He would love to see those. He would love to see his sister, Flare, and Amy. He thanks the Lord for protecting them and asks for His continued protection and provision on this trip. He asks for healing mercies for Marcus and thanks God that nothing worse happened to him. And he thanks his Heavenly Father for changing his heart toward Atlys. He doesn't see her the same way anymore. She's not the turncoat he thought she would be. Instead, she's...well, sort of nice, and definitely good with animals and medicine. She has her qualities. And, well, she's not terrible looking either...

Cornelius sits up straight. He hears voices. Yelling? He comes out of the bathroom as quickly as he can and leans out the window. Honestly, if he didn't know he was awake, he would think he was dreaming. This is it. This is what they've been waiting for, the moment they knew deep down would come. It's finally happening. They've been caught!

~ 17 ~

Cornelius is frozen at the window. He doesn't dare go out now, does he? There's a man yelling at Marcus. His hands are up in the air, and it appears he's calling for reinforcements on a radio.

Think, Corn, think! His inner voice sounds a lot like his sister, Flare.

Now Atlys is throwing her hands up too. She grabs Marcus by the back of his shirt and forces him to his knees. What in the world? Cornelius' mind is reeling. His heart is pounding! Every muscle in his body wants to crawl out this window or yell, but something holds him back.

And soon, he truly cannot believe his eyes. Atlys reaches into her backpack and pulls out a syringe. She moves over Marcus so quickly, she's a blur. When she comes back up, Marcus is holding his forehead. It's bleeding.

No.

No no no no no.

She can't be a GUY. She just CAN'T be!

The man radios again, but this time, begins slowly walking away. Atlys pulls Marcus to his feet by the back of his shirt again and begins dragging him away. The man disappears, off to patrol another area.

Atlys and Marcus are headed his way. What should he do?! Are they both GUYs now? He looks around and tries to find some way to protect himself. He runs to the kitchen and finds a meat tenderizer in a drawer. He notices the knives, but he just can't see him using it on his friends, even if they are now enemies. But even if Atlys is a GUY, Marcus just got his chip. There's still time to pull it out. He grabs for a small knife, just in case.

Cornelius hides behind the pantry door. Through the slats, he can see the window. It begins to open, and Marcus is crawling inside. Should he grab him and fight off Atlys?

There's no time to pray, but Cornelius says, "Lord, help me," then he crawls over to Marcus.

"Marcus? You okay?"

Marcus looks at him. There's blood dripping down his forehead.

"I'm so sorry! Quick, let's get it out!"

In a second, Cornelius is hovering over Marcus whose head is now on the carpet. His knife is poised over him an inch above his skin.

"What are you doing?" squeals Atlys, knocking Cornelius off of his friend. The knife flies out of his hand, and Cornelius scrambles to get it before she does. Except she's not going for it. She and Marcus watch Cornelius like he's a curiosity, like he's the freak show they just witnessed instead of the other way around.

"I'm fine," says Marcus, weakly. "Just nearly soiled my pants, that's all."

"What do you mean? Atlys, did you...are you..."

"That was for shooooow," says Atlys, drawing out the word into several syllables. "I didn't actually give Marcus a chip!"

"Then what?"

Marcus' voice is low and composed. "Atlys is a quick thinker. She just saved all our lives."

Cornelius looks between the faces of his two companions, back and forth, needing more information.

"I made him think I was a GUY and Marcus was already my capture," says Atlys. "When he was about to call in others, I made a big show of giving him a mark."

"But I just reached my fingers up my sleeve and grabbed some blood from my bullet wound," says Marcus. "When she came off me, I wiped my face with it."

"And it worked!" says Atlys, almost laughing. "I can't believe it worked!" Suddenly, her face contorts from a smile to a frown, and she begins to shake, crying softly.

"It's okay," says Marcus. "You were amazing. A star."

Cornelius sets the knife down and comes closer to Atlys. He sees her shaking and tries to put a hand to her shoulder to console her, but something holds him back here too. His emotions are raw. He's been utterly confused. His adrenaline is rushing through his system like wild, and he's unsure how to proceed. He has no idea how to feel right now.

"We're not leaving this house until after dark," says Marcus. "Sorry, folks, but I can't go through that again. Say, how is that toilet room? I think I'm the one who needs it now."

~ 18 ~

When the moon is bright, the three teens awake from naps in real beds and gather to head next door. There are no dogs here, so maybe, just maybe, they are both over there. It's worth a shot before heading back to the tunnels.

"Can't we sleep a little longer," asks Atlys, stretching her arms to the sides. That bed was incredible.

"I wish we could," says Marcus, "but it is best we do our moving in darkness."

"I know. You're right," she says. "I'm ready, I guess."

Cornelius hoists on his backpack, and they carefully unlock the back door, listening intently for any noise at all. "It's clear," he whispers.

They walk only a short bit through the yard to get to the other house. It looks nearly the same as the one they just left, so they head for the same window. Maybe it will grant them entry too.

Cornelius tries to open the window, but it won't budge. He moves down the back of the house to another window. No use. Breaking a window is not an option. It would call too much attention their way.

"I'm going to check the front of the house," says Atlys.

"Wait, we'll go—"

But Atlys is already gone. *Man, she's fast,* thinks Cornelius. He and Marcus sit as still as they can, hoping to hear footsteps inside the house or at least Atlys returning to them.

They wait.

And wait some more.

"Something is wrong," says Marcus. "She should be back by now. Let's go."

"Hold on," says Cornelius. He presses his ear against the window. "I think I hear something."

Another minute goes by and then they hear the distinct sound of the window lifting. It's Atlys! She made it in!

The boys crawl in without a word, passing their bags to Atlys. She stands there with a satisfied look on her face.

"Thanks," says Cornelius. "Any animals?"

"Afraid not," she says. Cornelius feels dejected. He's losing this battle. His one job is to bring the animals back, but if he can't find the animals, well, what's he doing out here, anyway? Risking his life? Their lives? Maybe it's time to pack it in and return to Heaventree.

The three move through the house stealthily and look for any signs of life. There are no animals here.

"Maybe we got the wrong house?" asks Marcus.

Cornelius opens his pack, removes his map and lays it over the coffee table. With a small flashlight, he looks over it carefully. "Look. We're here. These are the houses."

"All this for nothing," says Atlys. "Marcus got shot here!"

"And we nearly got caught," he adds.

"I just..." It occurs to him then. Cornelius has reached the end of himself. He's done everything he can think of to do to fulfill his quest, but it's not enough. It's time to hit his knees in prayer.

"Father God, we thank you and praise you for protecting us again and again. We want to do your will, but, Father, it seems we've come to a dead end. Without your help, we can't do any of this. Please guide us to where you want us to be. Help us find the pets we've been sent here to find so that your children will remain protected and hidden. In Jesus' name we pray. Amen."

The three teens sit on the sofa in silence, thinking over the day's events.

After a while, Marcus speaks up. "I guess it is time to return to the tunnel. Do you know what we are looking for this time?"

"I wish—I just wish we could sleep here," says Atlys. "I'm just so tired."

"We all are," says Cornelius, "but we can't chance it. We have to move at night from now on."

"I know you're right, but—"

"Let's just sit here for a little while longer," says Cornelius. Then at 1:00, we'll head out. Deal?"

"Sure," she says. "But you may have to wake me up." Atlys puts her head back on the sofa cushions and settles in.

Time moves slowly in the dark, and Marcus and Cornelius find that they are no longer tired, but acutely aware of their surroundings. They are rehearsing the moves they will take as they leave this safe house soon.

Sniff.

The boys' eyes open in the darkness.

Sniff sniff.

Marcus pokes Cornelius' leg. They sit up and listen.

Suddenly, they hear something moving. Outside the house? No. It's in this very room!

The boys stand and poise for action. Cornelius considers using his flashlight, but whatever is happening, he doesn't want them to be seen. They are sure now. They hear the unmistakable sounds of a dog. But how? How did they not see him?

In an instant, a wet nose finds its way to the three, nosing each one and wagging its tail. Atlys awakens and starts to speak, but Marcus shushes her. He pets the dog while Cornelius goes to where he thinks the dog came from. He feels around in the dark and nearly falls. There's a board moved! He reaches down.

"The floorboards," he whispers. "The dog was underneath."

"But...who let it out?" asks Marcus. Fear grips Cornelius and before he can move to safety, something emerges from the ground.

And this time, it's human.

~ 19 ~

Flare and Josh are sitting very still on the grass inside the Heaventree entrance. They've been there for a while. Flare wanted to get there early before the cart was retrieved and whatever animals Corn had saved were brought in. Josh didn't complain about getting up early. In fact, he didn't say much at all. Which is one of the reasons Flare is liking him more and more.

"I thought you were a real bonehead when I first met you," she says, pushing some dirt around with her finger.

"Oh yeah?" he asks. "Did I change your mind?"

"Sort of," says Flare, a slight grin forming. "What did you think of me?"

"Oooh, are you sure you want to ask that?"

"No," she says. "I take it back."

"You can't take it back now. It's already out there," Josh teases. "Well, let me see. We were in this tiny dark alleyway, pressed like sardines, and I heard this voice. Like an angel, really."

"You mean, freaking out," says Flare.

"Well, you're right. It wasn't an angel, it was a girl

totally freaking out. I guess, if I'm honest...I thought you were...a little bossy, maybe?"

Josh covers his head as if preventing an attack. But nothing comes. No arms, no fists from Flare. She just sits there, drawing in the dirt.

"You're not really bossy," he says, "I don't think you're—"

"Yes, I am," says Flare. "It's okay. I'm only like that because I've always felt protective over my brother. Always felt like he was younger and couldn't handle things on his own. And that day when you met us, I knew he was losing it. He gets really claustrophobic. Has panic attacks. And now...well, now I have no control over anything where he's concerned. Corn is out there, in danger, and with, who? Marcus is fine; I think he's a great guy, smart...I'm glad he's there. But Atlys? Really?"

"You don't agree with the group Mr. Deal put together?"

"I just don't trust her," says Flare. "None of us should. She showed her true colors last week in the house building contest."

"Speaking of houses," says Josh, "I need to get back soon and take care of the dogs in mine, or I'll have a whole lot more to clean up later."

"I'll come with you...I just need to see who Cornelius saved today. It makes me feel closer to him somehow."

"I'll wait a few more minutes," says Josh. And they sit in silence for what seems like forever.

Soon, Mr. Vollmer and Coach Arnold emerge from the

entrance. Flare jumps to her feet and brushes off the dirt and grass. She and Josh look behind the two mentors for the animals but none comes.

"Where are the pets?" asks Josh.

"Nothing came today," says Mr. Vollmer. "Except for these sleeping bags and supplies. Looks like they weren't picked up by our team." His face is dark with concern. Then he brightens. "I am sure it is nothing. Perhaps they were delayed in getting to the portal. I'm sure there is an easy explanation."

They walk on, a little quicker in step, leaning in and talking along the way.

"Hey, I—" Josh puts his arm on Flare's cast. "I'm sure they're fine."

But Flare shakes her head. She thinks of words to say, but nothing comes out. Her little brother is out there and in danger. She knows Atlys is going to turn on them, and now...now, her vision is coming true. She takes off running to go to the one place that can ease her worries. The Book of Martyrs. She has to see it. Has to make sure her brother isn't in it.

"I'll just..." Josh waves at Flare, long gone now, "see you later," he says. To no one.

Inside Castlebank, Flare opens the Book of Martyrs as carefully as she can. She wants to flip through quickly but realizes she may find something she doesn't want to see. What then? She works on her breathing. Slow it down, calm down. Taking her time, she looks through the names with one eye closed. She peeks at the pages then finds the last written entries. Here goes. She slowly skims down the page, taking note of the date. These are all from yesterday or today. There aren't so many, which is good, she thinks, and she doesn't recognize any names. Down, down, down, her eyes skim until...

He's not there. Cornelius is not there. He's alive!

Flare smiles and nearly feels like crying, she's so happy. She thanks the Lord for watching over her brother and then pushes up from her knees. She's going to help Josh with his animals. She is warmed from head to toe, thinking that her brother is safe and that she gets to go be with Josh. She turns and suddenly feels that she is not alone. Stiffening, Flare stops breathing for a second. Through the stained glass windows that flank the door, she sees a shadow. But it's low. Someone crouching?

Flare tiptoes to the doorway and just as she pokes her head out the door, she sees the back end of a black dog rounding the corner at the end of the hall. Why in the world is a dog in here? Flare wonders if it's the dog that's been hanging around Mr. Deal. Maybe he's here.

"Mr. Deal?" she calls out.

But no one answers. She calls out again. This time, a man clears his throat.

"Not Mr. Deal, just me."

It's Remley. He's carrying a box. "What you doing in there?" he asks.

"I just..." Flare stammers. "I could swear I just saw a dog in here."

"That black dog?" asks Remley. "Crazy dog pushed past

me when I came in the door," he says. "Shouldn't be dogs in this place. I was just trying to change a lightbulb. Where is it now?"

"Gone," says Flare. "Went that way."

"Well, I'll go make sure it's back outdoors. Yes sir. Leave it to me."

"Okay, well, see you later," says Flare. She realizes she is standing in front of the door to the room that holds the Book of Martyrs. Does Remley know about this book?

"Hope a dog's the most interesting thing you saw in here today," he says, purposefully holding her gaze and then eyeing the door behind her.

"It is," she says. Then with a slight smile she bids Remley good day.

Yep, he knows.

~ 20 ~

Cornelius, Marcus and Atlys are so still, they could be made of stone. They don't even breathe as the dog sniffs them. If they stay still in the darkness, maybe the person crawling up from the floor won't notice them until it's too late.

"Here boy," says the man. He clicks his tongue and the dog comes toward him. Cornelius' eyes sharpen in the dim glow coming from the moonlight. They make out the figure of a man, standing now. But the man stops.

No. He knows they're here!

Cornelius clutches at his side. He knows there's a knife in here somewhere, but nothing within his reach. He'll have to charge him. Here goes nothing. *Please God, protect us.*

One...two...

"Aaah!"

What the—

"Marcus!" says Atlys. Marcus rushes him first. The two are scuffling on the floor, and the dog is whimpering. Cornelius grabs for his backpack and finds the flashlight.

He throws a beam of light on the two wrestling on the floor. Finally, he says, "Marcus, stop!"

Marcus holds the man down on the ground by his shoulders. His arm is starting to bleed again through his bandages.

"Look, he has no mark."

Marcus looks intently at the man, breathing heavily, then leans back.

"Who are you?" he asks.

"Who are you?" asks the man, sitting up. The dog comes to him, wagging its tail.

"We're not GUYs," says Cornelius.

"We're not either," says the man.

"We? What do you mean...we?" asks Atlys.

"Are there more of you?" asks Cornelius, eying the floorboard.

"Please," says the man, catching his breath. "I need to know who you are."

Obviously he doesn't trust them. "We were sent by...Mr. Deal."

The man is silent and looks back and forth between the three teens. "Mr. Deal, as in...Heaventree?"

Cornelius takes a deep breath and smiles. "That's the one."

The man grabs at his heart and his face contorts. "Our children are at Heaventree. Is everything okay there?"

"Yes, we're all fine," says Cornelius. "Who are your children?"

"Well, I don't have any, per se, but..."

"There are others, aren't there," says Atlys. "Are they down there?" she says, pointing to the floor.

The man closes his eyes. "You haven't told me why you're here."

Cornelius looks to Marcus and then Atlys. He wants their approval before he talks. Marcus nods.

"We're..." begins Cornelius, "actually, we're looking for all the pets of the believers and rescuing them."

"Really?" says the man. "Why? I mean, that's incredible, but why would Mr. Deal send you kids out here, put you in danger, for...animals?" The dog comes and licks the man's face. "Don't get me wrong, I think it's awesome but—"

"The GU is using them to track down their owners in hiding. We save the animals, we protect the owners."

"Wow. Using the animals against us," says the man, rubbing his face. "How did you find this place? Are you sure you weren't followed?"

"It's on our list. We know where the Heaventree families lived and who had pets." Cornelius rifles through his backpack and pulls out his map. "This is supposed to be where...let's see...the Schultz family lives. This is Ryan Schultz' house. Are his parents down there with you?"

The man's eyes brighten. "You seem legit. And yes, they are. They're fine. Look...I pray I don't regret this, but...give me a minute to take the dog out and then I'll introduce you to...the others."

The man puts a leash around the dog's neck and heads to the back door. He peers out the windows first, then carefully unlocks the door and heads out into the nighttime.

Cornelius sits still, but his mind is whirling. Others, he said. There are others. Could his parents be here? Could he be just feet away from his mom and dad?

Tears well up in his eyes, and he wipes them. When he looks up he realizes that Atlys and Marcus are doing the same thing. They're all wondering, aren't they? They're all hoping to find their parents alive.

~ 21 ~

The Main Hall is humming with activity. Glasses and dishes are clanking, students are laughing and moving to the tables. Flare and Josh watch it all for a moment and then get in line for the food. It's sandwiches and soup today. They watch a couple boys carrying footlongs back to their seats.

"I have an idea," says Josh. He puts his hand on the small of Flare's back, and she turns.

"Let's have a picnic."

"A picnic," says Flare. Her face breaks out into a full-on smile. "Really?"

"Really," says Josh, his eyebrow rising. "I just thought, you know, if it's stuff we can eat with our hands...why not go outside and...maybe watch the construction going on in the lake?"

"That's not a half-bad idea," says Flare, feeling her face flush. She bites her lip and then says, "but what about Amy? If she gets here and we're not here...well, I just don't want her to eat alone."

"She can come too," says Josh.

"Yeah, okay, then." They move slowly through the line,

and Flare keeps her eye on the door, waiting for Amy to enter. But she never does. By the time they get their food, Flare says, "Grab one more for Amy. I'm going to go look for her. She's usually here by now."

Josh carries the three wrapped up sandwiches under his arm and says, "I'll meet you out at the picnic tables, I guess. Hurry back. I'm hungry."

Flare catches his eye and holds his gaze. She smiles and then heads back to Chizoba Hall. Maybe Amy's still in their room.

"Amy?" Flare says as she opens her door. "You in here?"

She's met with nothing but silence. The room is dark, so Flare goes to the window to open the curtains and let some light in. She looks behind her and sees Amy's form lying on her bed. Maybe she's taking a nap?

Flare moves closer and hovers over Amy's face to see if she's awake or not. She moves her hand over her eyes.

"I'm awake, you know," says Amy.

"Oh," says Flare. "I just...wondered where you were. We were getting lunch and you never came. You feeling okay?"

"Mmm," she murmurs, indicating she is not that good.

"Well, do you need to go to the infirmary?"

"It's not like that. I'm just...sad." She sighs.

Flare sits down on the edge of the bed. "I know you are. And I'm sorry. You have every right to be sad. I just...well, I miss you. I know you're still here and all, but I miss, well, your smile and you know, all the good times."

"Sorry to be such a damper for you." Amy rolls over and away from Flare.

"No, no, it's not that at all. I totally understand, I just, well, I wanted you to know...I wish I could help you. That's all. I'm praying for you, but I wish there was something more I could do. If I could take your pain away, I would."

"Funny," says Amy. "That's what my mother would say when something bad would happen." The room goes quiet. "Then she'd say that the Lord is close to the brokenhearted. She'd say to use those times I was sad to lean into the Lord."

"Your mother sounds really wise."

"She was." Amy rolls over and sits up, resting her hands on her knees.

Flare is suddenly struck with an idea. She stands and heads to her own bed. She reaches into her nightstand and pulls out a locket. It's the locket Miss Carmine had been wearing, the one Flare found in the hospital. She holds it in her hands and feels the duplicate locket around her neck. She rubs it and remembers Miss Carmine. She thinks she would approve.

"I want you to have this," says Flare. She hands her the necklace. "It's a two-way radio. It works with mine. We can talk to eachother on it. You can...get me whenever you need me."

Flare's eyes tear up as Amy pulls her hair to the side so Flare can put it on her. When it's clasped, Amy wraps her arms around her friend and they just sit there for a minute.

Pulling away, Flare lifts her locket and says, "Testing, testing..."

Her voice comes out in Amy's locket and Amy jumps. Then laughs. "Hey, this is pretty cool."

"I know," says Flare. "Use it whenever you want."

Amy lifts her locket to her mouth and says, "I'm hungry."

The girls giggle and they head out together to find Josh, three sandwiches, and a picnic table by the lake.

~ 22 ~

"This is so exciting," whispers Atlys. "I can't believe we found more believers! Maybe we should, I dunno, bring them back with us to Heaventree."

Cornelius' heart stills. That's not at all what he was asked to do. He had one task, finding the animals and rescuing them.

But actually, that's not all. There was something else he was supposed to do. R & R, he remembers Mr. Deal saying. Rescue and Reconnaissance. They've done great at the rescue part, but the reconnaissance, the information, the spying part? Not so much. Maybe these undergrounders have information they can take back with them to Heaventree.

But taking back people? No. Unless…

Cornelius thinks about his parents again. Are they down there? Where is that guy and the dog? Shouldn't they be back by now?

The door creaks open and all three teens perk up, hoping it's the man they talked to and not some intruder. The dog assuages their fear. It bounds in and licks Cornelius' face.

"Okay, boy," he says. The man behind him shuts and locks the door, then crawls down to the floor where Marcus, Atlys and Cornelius are sitting. "You three...you ready? God help me if you aren't who you say you are."

"Same," says Marcus. "We each must trust the other."

"Well then." The man begins lifting up the floorboards and the dog leads the way to the hideaway down below.

Cornelius doesn't know what he was expecting, but he wasn't expecting to be in a small underground tunnel with no lights. It makes sense, of course it does, but he begins to feel his throat constricting. He pulls at his hoodie to try to get some air, then he touches the cold earth walls beside him. He tries hard not to think about his claustrophobia threatening to overtake him. A verse from Psalm 55 comes to him:

My heart pounds in my chest, the terror of death assaults me. Fear and trembling overwhelm me, and I can't stop shaking.

Oh, that I had wings like a dove; then I would fly far away to the quiet of the wilderness.

"Wings like a dove?" says Atlys.

Was he saying that out loud? He thought it was only in his head! Cornelius is getting dizzy.

"Breathe, man," says Marcus. And Cornelius breathes.

Soon, a light begins to illuminate the way up ahead. He focuses on it like a laser beam, feeling the sweat on his hands now. He's almost there. Almost there.

And when the light grows brighter, the man and the dog round the corner and the three teens are left, mouths gaping, standing in the entryway of a large room filled with people. It only takes seconds before Atlys shrieks and runs to hug someone she obviously knows very well.

"Uncle Jase!" Atlys hugs his neck so tight and so long, he begins to crumple. "Where's Mom and Dad?" she asks.

Cornelius and Marcus watch as the man grabs a chair for Atlys and has her sit. They can't hear what he's saying, but by the look on Atlys' face, something must be wrong.

Marcus begins to scan the room. This is no dull crowd; there are people of all races, of all nationalities here, wrapped in scarves and bright colors. The torch lights flicker and cast lively shadows that dance across a sea of faces.

Cornelius feels Marcus get pulled in and in a moment, he is deep in the crowd.

We're all searching, hoping, thinks Cornelius. *Maybe Mom and Dad are here after all.* Heart beginning to pound again, Cornelius moves toward a splash of red hair across the room. It's there, then gone again. He almost won't allow himself to hope it's his mother. If it's not, it may crush him.

Allow yourself to hope, he hears the Holy Spirit whisper, but as he touches the woman's arm and she turns, he cannot help but feel let down.

"I—I was just looking for someone," he mumbles. "Your hair...I thought you might be her."

"Hair like mine? That's a bit unusual," says the woman, her thin lips curling into a smile. "But I have seen someone else here with the same color."

"Really?" beams Cornelius. "Where? Which way?"

"Well, she was here," says the woman, "but she left a couple days ago. A group went out, foraging for food and supplies. I think. I remember she was with them. Not sure if it was your mother though."

"She may have been with my father. He has brown hair...a lot like mine. Their name is Flanagan."

The woman eyes Cornelius hard and begins to nod. "Yes, maybe so."

"Who's in charge here?" asks Cornelius.

"Salem," she says, looking around. "He's...that one there, with the white hair and ponytail."

The old man is talking with Marcus. Looks like he had the same idea. Cornelius begins to move toward them when he turns and says, "Thanks," to the red-haired woman.

She smiles. "I'm sorry I wasn't your mother. I can see you're a very nice boy."

As Cornelius approaches Salem and Marcus, Atlys draws near too. Her eyes, slightly puffy now from tears, are firmly on this long-haired man. "We're looking for our parents," she says. "I know mine were here."

"Is that why you came?" asks Salem, looking from one teen to the next and finally resting on Cornelius.

"Well, no, not exactly," he tells him. "But at the moment, it's pretty high on our list. It seems we may have just missed them. Please, sir, tell us what you know."

"First, I must understand who you are. Where you come from. What you are doing here."

Cornelius turns and looks at Marcus, searching his eyes. Should they discuss Heaventree at all? Marcus seems to read his mind and nods slightly. "We come from a special school...it's been less than two weeks since we first arrived, but then this war began. So we were sent out to search for pets of believers, of non-GUYs, and bring them back with us. It's all to protect, well, people like you down here, I guess. To keep GUYs from finding you."

"Yet you found us. Didn't you."

"O-on accident. We just knew where the houses were. We were searching for a couple of dogs—"

"We've brought down a few ourselves," says Salem. "It makes the underground a little more bearable for some."

"So our parents," says Cornelius. "Are they here? Are all the believers here or are they scattered about?"

"They are not all here, no," says Salem. He laughs, "That would be impossible. You see, the resistance is growing." He turns to the crowd and spreads his right arm out over them. "Tell me, uh, what is your name?"

"Cornelius."

"Cornelius, tell me, how does a virus work?"

"A virus? It invades the body and makes you sick."

"By multiplying and spreading," adds Atlys.

"Precisely. And are you aware that the Global Union views you and I and all of us here as a virus that must be eliminated?"

"A virus, sir?" says Cornelius.

"Indeed. Now, if we stay in one sheltered place and protect ourselves, are we multiplying and spreading?"

"I—I suppose if people have children they would multiply..."

"How else?" asks Salem. "How might the Spirit of the Truth spread to others?"

"Evangelism," says Atlys. "Spreading the Good News."

"Spreading it to who, exactly?" says Cornelius. "GUYs? That's crazy."

"Is it?" Salem beckons for a young black woman to come close. When she is a couple feet away, they can all see it. She has a bloody bandage on her forehead. "Chandra, please tell these good people how you came to be here."

The woman's face erupts into a huge smile. "These crazy brave people, they told me about Jesus. They explained how we could be filled with true life instead of the constant downloads of the GU. But I didn't want to hear it. Not at first. In fact, I considered turning them in."

"But you didn't?" asks Atlys.

"I was about to, but in my second encounter, they said that removing my chip would allow me to think for myself and that if I wanted to put it back in, I could do it. I decided I had nothing to lose. When my chip was gone, it was as if I was seeing the world for the very first time. I was free." Her eyes water and she rubs her bandage slightly. "I can never thank them enough."

"Are they here?" asks Marcus. "The people who did this. Did they bring you here?"

"They brought me here, yes, but then they left. I assume to help others."

"Do you know their names?"

"Not all of them, but I remember one. She had the most brilliant hair I've ever seen."

Cornelius gulps. "Red?" he asks timidly.

"Red, yes! Flanagan was her name. She and her husband, they saved my life. They saved my very soul."

Marcus and Atlys instinctively embrace Cornelius as his knees grow weak and his heart floods. His parents are alive, and more than that, they're risking their lives to save people. Although time and space are between them now, Cornelius has never felt more connected to his parents than he does at this very moment. And it makes his longing to see his sister, Flare, nearly unbearable. He cannot wait to tell her the news.

~ 23 ~

Flare is praying. It's not as if she's on her knees with eyes closed or anything, rather she has a paintbrush in her hands and is swirling colors on a canvas. With each stroke, a silent yet deep felt muttering is offered to God. It's a partnership, this creative prayer. He tells her where to put her colors, and she pours out her worries and fears. *Take care of my brother, You are all powerful, God, watch over our parents, Your will be done, protect Heaventree*, and on and on. When the painting is complete—an abstract with dark vertical lines, a red circle and yellow swooshes—Flare knows the cracks in the dome are healed. How she knows, she doesn't quite understand. But she remembers Miss Carmine's notes. She hopes she's making her proud. She'd do anything to honor the memory of her mentor.

Flare is just sticking her brush into a jar of water when Joe and Nattie walk up. They brought a cool breeze with them, and the wind blows her red hair toward the lake.

"Hey," says Joe. "You know where Josh is?"

"I'm not his keeper," says Flare. "but...I imagine he's in his house, walking dogs or something."

"We looked and he wasn't—"

Nattie interrupts. "Mr. Deal needs him."

"For what?" asks Flare.

"I thought you weren't his keeper," Joe snips.

"Very nice," Flare says. She wipes her hands on a rag and starts to pick up her painting and easel. She pours the painty water into the grass.

"We're working on the treehouse," says Nattie. "It's amazing, really. I've been assisting Mr. Vollmer on some mathematical equations...honestly, some I've never even seen before. They don't even make sense."

"Not sure you're making sense right now," says Flare.

"What she means is, this is no ordinary treehouse," says Joe. "I've been working on building it with the other guys, and Nattie's been coming up with calculations and proportions, but apparently Josh's muscles or whatever is needed to finish the job."

Flare looks from one face to the other, then picks up her things. "Let me put this away and I'll go look for him with you. I kinda want to see this treehouse myself."

"Yeah and maybe Josh's muscles too?"

"Seriously?" Flare pushes the side of Joe's head and says, "Let's just go." She puts her head down and lets her hair cover her face. She can feel the redness in her cheeks. How can just talking about Josh have that effect?

Flare, Joe and Nattie walk back toward Chizoba Hall first. "What are you going to do with all those paintings?" asks Joe. "You're going to have a gazillion soon."

"Mr. Deal is putting them somewhere, not sure where. I leave them in our meeting space in Chizoba, and every now and then someone picks them up."

"We could hang them in the houses we built," says Joe. "Would be nice to have something on the walls. The dogs and cats would love it."

After dropping off the art, the three walk toward the lake. There's a slow rolling fog beginning to move across it, closer to them. The treehouse is partly obscured, but what is visible is...

"Wow," says Flare.

"Yeah," says Joe.

"Look how high that thing goes!"

"I know," says Nattie. It's up about twenty stories high."

"How can that tree possibly hold it?" Flare asks. "It looks like it's floating or something."

"You should see the inside."

"How in the world are you building this so fast?"

"The same way we built six houses in six days, I guess," says Joe.

"And Mr. Vollmer is taking the lead on this," says Nattie. "He's not a builder, but a mathematician, and he's engineered something really mind-blowing." She turns her head and stares at the treehouse then lowers her eyes. "He just won't tell us what it's for."

"Wait, you mean you two are working on this thing, and he won't even tell you what it's for?"

"Is that so strange?" asks Joe. "Mr. Deal didn't tell us what our houses were for until they were finished. Maybe they'll do the same with this."

"Do the same with what?" Flare turns at the familiar voice. Josh is standing behind them, nearly breathing over Flare's shoulder. She closes her eyes.

"Oh, there you are," says Nattie. "Mr. Deal is looking for you."

"For me?" says Josh, rubbing his chest and scratching.

"He needs help with the treehouse or something," says Joe.

"Right now?" Josh looks at his watch. "I've got to walk the dogs soon."

"He's up there," says Joe, pointing to the treehouse. "You have to go that way around the lake. There's a boat that takes you over.

Josh throws his hands up then takes off running in that direction. Flare, Nattie and Joe stand motionless and in awe as they try to make sense of the treehouse proportions. It just doesn't seem like it's physically possible.

This is where faith comes in. The thought is almost audible in her head, and it sounds just like her mother. Flare's heart swells, praying her parents and brother are safe, and she thinks about the invisible dome protecting them all here at Heaventree. She doesn't understand it or the treehouse, but then again, God doesn't require her understanding of things. Only her faith in Him.

~ 24 ~

"We've been here too long," says Marcus. He comes close to Cornelius and leans back against the wall. The two watch the stream of people moving around them in the underground bunker.

"We haven't seen our parents yet. I mean, I haven't. Atlys hasn't." Cornelius is quiet, wishing he hadn't said those things. Marcus doesn't know where his mother is. No one has seen her.

"Did we finish our mission?" Marcus asks. "Did we retrieve all of the animals that were on our list...that we could, anyway?"

"We have, but...what about the information we're supposed to come home with? What do we have to tell Mr. Deal that he doesn't already know?"

The woman with the bandage over her head walks by, talking with another in a brightly colored dress.

"Well," says Marcus, "we know about this place. We know there is a group of believers who are hiding underground. We know that this is not the only group. Salem said the resistance was growing. We also know there are converts being made daily."

"Yes, but what about the Global Union? We don't know what it's doing, what it's planning."

"I do," says Atlys. She appears next to Cornelius and slides down the wall to sitting. He joins her there, knees in front of his face. "My uncle told me what he's heard," she says. "The GU is going to ban all forms of currency, all money. The only way to buy or sell anything will be digitally...through the mark. Anyone who doesn't have one can't buy anything. No food, nothing."

The three are quiet for a moment, letting that sink in. "It's not as if they aren't underground already, hiding, living in fear," says Cornelius.

"Yes, and not as if they aren't being hunted and killed already," says Marcus.

"But all these people, all their money, all their wealth and valuables they've gathered their whole lives...it all means nothing." Atlys leaves her hands hanging in the air.

"Can't take it with you," says Marcus.

Cornelius feels a wave of homesickness. He misses his dog, Pepper. He misses the quiet days at home, lying on his bed, reading a book, listening to his mother hum as she gardened. He misses his Dad telling dad jokes. He misses Flare bossing him around. He presses his hands on his knees and moves to standing. "It's time to go back to Heaventree," he says. Marcus nods.

"I'll let Salem know," says Marcus.

"No," says Atlys. "Our parents aren't back yet. I'm not going anywhere."

The three instinctively watch the doorway they entered

when they first arrived. They've each been eyeing it periodically, hoping to see a familiar face come through.

"We can't leave you here, Atlys," says Cornelius.

"I don't want to stay here," she says. "I want to go back to Heaventree, just with my parents. It's safer there."

"I—I don't think that's what the plan was," says Cornelius. "I don't think we were supposed to bring back people...only pets."

Atlys shoots up and gets in Cornelius' face. "You are such a rule follower," says Atlys. "Everything you do...Mr. Deal said this, or Mr. Deal said we can't do that! When are you going to think on your own for a change?" Atlys storms off into the crowd, and Marcus and Cornelius are left with their eyebrows raised in disbelief.

Cornelius can feel his throat constricting. He doesn't just follow rules, he tries to do what's right. He suddenly feels the earth above him. He's trapped underground. Can't breathe. He closes his eyes and clenches his fists. He tries to picture his sister calming him down. Tries to remember her face, but it seems blurry...he can't make out her features, only her red hair. He thinks he might faint. He thinks—

Cornelius wakes up in a small earthen room, a cave off of the main room. His backpack is beneath his head. He turns and sees a man; it's Salem. He's sitting beside him, holding something.

Cornelius reaches back and feels the top of his backpack. It's not there.

The book!

"I see you've come around," says Salem. "That's good. You scared your friend, Marcus, quite a bit."

Cornelius sits and reaches for the book. "Sir, that's mine."

"Is it?" asks Salem. "I was hoping you would say that because...well, I was curious and tried to open it. Strangely, this book will not open for me. Do you happen to know why?"

"Because it's not your book?" says Cornelius, totally uneasy. He might throw up.

Salem smiles. He hands the book back to Cornelius. "There now," he says. "Go ahead. You open it if it is yours."

"I can't," says Cornelius.

"Can't... or won't?" asks Salem, eyeing him through slitted lids.

"Both," says Cornelius. "It's meant for someone else. I-I was asked to deliver it, not open it."

"And what happens if you open it? Will you turn into a pillar of salt like Lot's wife? Will you be jailed? Oh, wait, that could happen easily these days."

"I'm not sure what will happen," says Cornelius, taking the book and turning to put it back in his pack. "But I'm just doing what I was told."

"You do what you're told, do you?" Salem begins to laugh, and somehow his tone changes to not so friendly anymore. "Do you think any of us got here by doing what we were told? Do you think I became the leader of a growing resistance because I follow rules and orders? Now, give me that book, and open it for me."

Cornelius eyes the doorway. His head is still woozy, but he knows enough to get out of here. In a flash, he throws the book under his shirt and runs past the old man. Marcus sees him running and goes after him. By the time they are in the entryway, Cornelius pants, "Atlys!"

"She's not coming. She refuses."

Cornelius is torn. He knows they can't stay here, not as long as he has this book in his possession. What is the book, anyway? And why does Salem want it?

"Cornelius," says Marcus, placing his hand on his wrist. "Why are you running?"

"Salem. He's changed. He's, I don't know...something's not right."

"Then we must go now," says Marcus. "Without her. We can come for her later."

Torn, the two boys wind their way through the underground and make it back to the entrance. It's dark except for a sliver of light above. Cornelius presses up on the floorboards to the house they once entered looking for a dog. They found so much more here. So much more.

Wasting no time in case they were followed, Marcus and Cornelius head out into the night in silence, thinking of all they have seen and heard, praying for Atlys and all the believers underground. Everytime he sees humans, instead of averting his eyes, Cornelius keeps his open, hoping to catch a glimpse of his mother, a swath of red hair. It's this that keeps him going through the night until they finally find the portal, a small rotten treehouse in the back of a deserted home. As they crawl up into it and close the door behind them, they are suddenly in the tunnel again. The railcar is waiting.

Cornelius has never been so happy to see this cramped place. It means the next stop is Heaventree — the closest thing he has to home.

~ 25 ~

It's been six days since Cornelius has been gone. Flare kicks the dirt in the early morning light, waiting at the entrance to Heaventree. Amy is beside her, silent. They feel too afraid to speak. Yesterday, they stood here eager to see what animals Cornelius, Marcus and Atlys sent through, but nothing came. After 62 pets and one stray black dog, nothing came from the outside.

Flare's heart had sunk. Something must be wrong, she thought. She'd looked over toward Mr. Deal to read his face. He simply rubbed his cheeks and readjusted his ballcap. The black dog sat at his side, panting expectantly, but eventually lay down, tired of waiting.

This morning, the dog is here again, but Mr. Deal is not, which is strange, Flare thinks. Mr. Vollmer, Madame Dubose and Professor Moss are sipping coffee, chatting about the newly constructed treehouse. These morning gatherings ebb and flow with people eager to see the newest rescued pets.

After waiting for nearly an hour, the girls hear something. Amy grabs Flare's arm and squeezes. Flare can feel her heart pounding out of her chest. Maybe they're fine after all. Maybe yesterday was just a slow day when they didn't find any pets. What will they see today? Dogs? Cats? Another ferret?

"Cornelius!" Flare screams. She runs toward her brother and nearly knocks him down. He drops his backpack and hugs her hard. She's crying now, and so is he. Flare backs up and looks at him. "You're here! You're really here."

"I'm really here," he says, wearily. Cornelius looks around and sees Amy. She comes close slowly and hugs him at his side.

"Don't get too close," he says sheepishly. "Haven't seen a shower in days." He wipes his eyes as if unsure of what he's actually seeing. "Boy, it's great to see you guys. I can't tell you what this week's been like."

"But you have to!" squeals Flare as she grabs his hand. "You have to tell us everything!"

Cornelius looks behind him and spots Marcus, lumbering in on tired legs. Cornelius goes to him and puts his hand out. They shake hands hard and end in a strong hug on Marcus' good side. No words are needed between these two friends. Flare watches their exchange and knows these boys have been through a lot.

But where's Atlys? Flare's throat clenches. "Corn? Where's Atlys?"

Cornelius looks at Marcus, and he answers, "She's safe. For now."

"But why didn't she come back with you?" asks Amy.

"I'm afraid that's a long story," says Cornelius.

"Well then, you'd better get started," says Flare. Visions of the drawing she made of Atlas flood her mind. Did she abandon them for the Global Union? Did she turn on them and become a GUY?

"Someone needs to start explaining where Atlys is," says Professor Moss, bullish and standing ground. "Where is your teammate? You were supposed to look out for one another! How could you leave--"

"We said she's safe!" says Cornelius, exasperated.

"Wait just a moment," says Madame Dubose. "These boys need to rest. And get looked at in the infirmary." She grabs Marcus's hand and begins to pull him toward her. His bloody bandage has dried stiff against his side.

"Maybe she's right," says Marcus. "Let us go get cleaned up. We can see our friends...and family...soon. And we can explain everything then."

And just like that, the boys hoist their bags on their backs and follow the tiny Madame Dubose and Mr. Vollmer toward the infirmary while Professor Moss storms off. Flare feels her cast on her left arm and remembers her own stay there. Was it just a week ago? How is so much happening so fast? Is it possible time is moving faster now?

Seeing her scruffy-haired little brother walking off, looking more like a foot soldier than a kid, suddenly the tears well up in her eyes and Flare cannot control them any longer. *Thank you, God, for bringing him back safely. Thank you, thank you, thank you...*Flare feels her prayers of thanks will never cease.

In the infirmary, the nurse removes Marcus' bloody bandage on his arm and eyes his wound. "You were shot, all right, but it's not in there. In fact, this looks really good, considering. Who cleaned you up?"

"Atlys," he says.

"Well, you need to thank your friend. This could have been...and gotten...much worse than it did."

Atlys. Hearing her name hurts Cornelius to his core. How could he have left her? He feels a rush of adrenaline and wants to run back out there. He's seen his sister is safe, but he shouldn't have left one of their own. This was his responsibility. Cornelius moves toward the door and looks out, thinking of running.

But he's met with the gaze of Mr. Deal in the hallway, hands clasped in front of him.

"I see you made it back," says Mr. Deal. A slight smile forms in the edges of his mouth. "It's good to see you. I'm amazed you saved so many pets...and even more amazed you're still alive."

"You...*you* sent me out there. Sent *us*."

"I know, I'm just kidding. I'm not surprised you're alive, just very...proud of you." Mr. Deal puts his hand on Cornelius' shoulder. He stares into his eyes. "But I understand Atlys did not make it back."

"She's okay, sir, she just...chose not to come back yet. It-it's complicated."

"Then I suggest you come with me and tell me all about it. It does not seem like you to leave a teammate in the wild. I would say I am disappointed in you, except that...I know Atlys as well. So come, let's talk."

Cornelius grabs his backpack from the floor and carries it, feeling its weight. The whole reason he had to flee so quickly and leave his friend is because of the book in his pack, the book meant only for Mr. Deal.

What in the world could be in it that's so important?

In Mr. Deal's office, Cornelius sits where he sat just a week ago. Funny, he feels a lot older.

Mr. Deal settles across from him and cracks his knuckles. "Now then, where is Atlys?"

"We found...well, one of the houses we were supposed to go to had a hidden underground passageway beneath it. Long story short, we found a whole group of believers hiding there. Atlys' uncle was there. He said her parents had been there but were out for a while. She didn't want to leave without them."

"I see. An underground cell. How many people were there?" he asks.

"Too many to count," says Cornelius. "And apparently it's growing. There are some people there who are helping to convert GUYs, removing their chips and sharing the gospel."

Mr. Deal smiles.

"In fact, sir, my parents are some of those people."

"I see," says Mr. Deal. "Did you see them?"

"No. I had to leave before they came back."

Mr. Deal leans forward. "You had to leave? Why?"

Cornelius fidgets and lifts his foot on his knee, playing with a shoelace. "There was this guy there, this old man named Salem."

Mr. Deal stiffens.

"He seems to be the leader there, or something. Anyway, he got his hands on a book I have—"

"A book?" asks Mr. Deal.

"Yeah." Cornelius leans over to open his backpack and

carefully puts the book in his lap. It's still wrapped in brown paper and twine. "It-it's for you, actually. The man at Leaf Bookstore told me to give it to you."

"Mr. Chang," says Mr. Deal, his eyes lighting up. He reaches his hand out and Cornelius slowly places the book in his hands. Cornelius waits for him to open it, but he doesn't. He just rubs every inch of it, turning it over and back again. "Mr. Chang and I go way back," he says finally. "When I was much younger we had wonderful conversations about literature, philosophy, prophecy. I'm glad to hear he's all right."

Cornelius bites his lip. "Sir? What's in the book? The old man, Salem, tried to open it and it wouldn't open for him. He got angry and—"

"Ah yes, Salem Scathe," says Mr. Deal. "Of course he would be after this book." Mr. Deal stands and walks to the window, clutching the book to his chest. "Salem is a preacher. A very good one. He grew a large following and was, well, on a watchlist for the GU. When I had my chip I became aware of him, and even listened to some of his sermons by radio transmission." He turns and rubs his chin, eying the ground. "But even people with great motives, great hearts, can be led astray by their own ambitions. Men aren't made to be praised; we're not gods. After a while, if a Christian leader is not careful, he or she may become like the Pharisees and begin placing themselves in the seats of honor."

"And you think Salem is this way?" asks Cornelius.

"I think so, yes," says Mr. Deal. "When I was going to build this school, he caught wind and wanted to be involved. But his involvement seemed more about him and less about what Christ was doing. He even wanted Heaventree to be named after him."

"Scathetree?"

"Not exactly, but something like that."

Cornelius is quiet, replaying the scene with Salem in his mind. He jolts to standing. "Sir? Will you...open the book?"

"It will be opened, yes," he says.

"But just not with me here," says Cornelius, dejected.

"Tell you what," says Mr. Deal. "I promise to tell you if and when you need to know."

"Gee, thanks." Cornelius is suddenly exhausted and ravenous. When was the last time he had an actual meal? Mr. Deal catches him by the arm as he heads for the door.

"Cornelius, I am beyond grateful that you were such a good steward of this book and of your mission. I knew you were the man for the job."

"At times I wasn't so sure," says Cornelius. "Like Marcus getting shot. And leaving Atlys. Sir, we need to go back and get her."

"We will," says Mr. Deal. "Let's just give her a day or two with her family. In the meantime, you might want to go take a look at the houses of Heaventree. I think you'll like what you see."

~ 26 ~

Flare's heart is full. They're home. She's watching Marcus get examined by a doctor and feeling as if her heart may burst with happiness. She had no idea how much she'd missed Cornelius. She must have locked away that emotion in a place that made it more bearable to get through each day without him. Perhaps it's the same place she holds her memories of her parents.

Nope, that hurts. She still can't go there.

"I'm going to go for a walk," she tells Amy. She lifts her locket. "Let me know when Marcus is free to leave."

"Okay," Amy says. Marcus smiles and kicks his feet off the end of the examination table.

On some level, Flare knows where she's heading, but she's not fully conscious of it until she reaches her house, the House of Flare. It's basically a cat house now. There are three cats sleeping in the front, one gray, one calico, and one just really round. They seem to care less if she comes near or not. Flare opens the door slowly and marvels again at the handiwork of her friends. *We built this,* she thinks, *with our own hands.*

"So you would have a place to sleep," she tells an

orange tabby, lying in a spot of sunshine by the window. There are literally cats and kittens everywhere.

Flare sits on the floor to let a small black cat with a white tuft of fur at his neck come crawl across her lap. He bounces and purrs and soon falls asleep. It's so peaceful here. *Oh, to have the life of a cat,* she thinks. *No worries. No war going on.*

She strokes his little head and he stirs. Someone's coming in.

"He—hey," says Josh. "What are you doing here?"

"In my own house?" she says slyly.

"You know what I mean," he says. "You come to change the litter boxes?"

"I'm pretty sure that's your job," she says.

"Well, I've delegated that one to Evan. It's the sign of a good leader to delegate."

Josh sits cross-legged beside Flare on the ground, but it looks awkward with his knees sticking up.

"I just like sitting with the cats," says Flare. "They feel safe here. See how they get along? Can you imagine what Cornelius and Marcus and Atlys had to do to get them here? Can you even imagine?"

"Honestly, I can't," says Josh. He looks up and sees Flare's eyes begin to shine. "You okay?"

"Yes. He's home, you know."

"I heard. That's awesome news."

The door creaks open. "Did someone say awesome news?"

"Cornelius!" Josh yells. He jumps up and ruffles his

hair, pushing him back. "Good to see you, man! How in the world are you?!"

The kitten in Flare's lap jumps off and runs toward the back of the house. Cornelius' eyes light up as he walks around and sees cats literally everywhere. He rubs one on the head, and his face breaks out into a wide grin. He turns to his sister. "Oh my gosh," he says.

"Yeah," she says. "Looks like you were busy."

Josh watches him for a while then says, "Come on. Wanna show you something." They follow Josh out the door, down the path and to another house. It's Josh's house. They open the door and several little dogs and a couple large ones bark and run to the teens, jumping up on Cornelius. As he's licked in the face and hands, he laughs and turns to Flare. She's smiling but tears are running down her face.

"I remember you!" he says. "Hey, buddy, I remember you, too!"

Flare bursts into the mix and hugs her little brother hard then helps settle the dogs as they walk them to the fenced backyard and let them run, run, run.

"I've been in charge of caring for all these critters," says Josh, arms crossed and head cocked back. "Pretty much a nonstop job. Thanks so much. I think I would have preferred being out there with you, rescuing them all, risking life and limb."

Cornelius nods and purses his lips. He remembers each one of the animals, remembers the darkness, the danger, the close calls and getaways. Remembers the break-ins and missed chances. Mostly he remembers Marcus and Atlys, seeing their faces, being grateful he wasn't out there alone.

He remembers Atlys. *God, is she safe? Are you protecting her still?*

His stomach turns and he grabs it, feeling ill.

"Have you eaten?" asks Flare? "The Main Hall's open."

Cornelius leans down to let a little Yorkie jump up on his knee. He pets her head and stands. "Lead the way. I'd eat anything they put in front of me. Then I want a shower. And a bathroom in general. And a bed."

Flare puts her arm in his and they head off toward the Main Hall, Josh in tow. Flare feels like she can't get close enough to her brother. He's here, at her side, but something in his mind is keeping him far, far away. She prays they can get some time alone and he can finally open up and bring her in. Right before they walk in the door, the girls in the House of Flare show up and start fawning over her brother. Flare realizes it might be harder than she thought to get some time alone with Corn. He's practically a celebrity now.

~ 27 ~

In the dark hours of the morning, Cornelius lies awake. Now that he's in his soft bed, clean and fed, he worries about Atlys. He replays every single day of their past week together. He's been with Marcus and Atlys every second of those days and nights and now...it feels as if he's missing something. He wants to find Marcus. Needs to see him. He's the only one who truly knows what it was like out there. He's the only one who can understand how it feels to have left Atlys behind.

Cornelius sits up and hears Joe snoring softly in the other bed. He reaches blindly for his shorts and pulls them on. Same goes with his hoodie. Stepping into some slides, he carefully opens the door. As soon as he turns and shuts it behind him, something grabs him.

"Ah!" he squeals.

"Shhh, it's just me." It's his sister, Flare.

"What are you doing?"

"What are *you* doing? I was coming to see you."

"What about? I was...going to find Marcus."

"Well, we haven't had a chance to talk, really," says Flare, leaning out over the railing and looking toward the lake. The moon barely lights the water. "Not alone, anyway."

Cornelius feels a prick of guilt. He shares everything with his sister. But this last week was different. She wasn't there.

"Come on," says Cornelius. "Let's go for a walk before Mr. Deal wakes everybody up."

Cornelius and Flare make their way downstairs and out the door of Chizoba Hall. Then they just keep walking, aimlessly. Their eyes begin to adjust to the darkness just about the time Cornelius is explaining how they prayed to the Lord for the crowd to be blinded and then got away with the giant mastiff, Wally.

"No way!" says Flare. "He's the sweetest dog ever. Huge! I can't believe that happened."

Suddenly, an alarm sounds, and Cornelius grabs his sister's shoulder.

Weeeeee-ooo-weeeeee-ooo-weeeeee...

"What in the world?"

Intruder alert. Intruder alert.

"Intruder? Quick, this way," says Cornelius. He may be at Heaventree, but his instincts are still raw from being on the outside, in danger all the time. Cornelius grabs his sister's hand, and they run toward the entrance. Maybe it's just Atlys. Maybe she came home alone! He's hoping so.

People are scrambling and yelling now near the entrance. The teens can't quite make out anyone's faces, but after a struggle and someone falling to the ground, things quiet down a bit, and a group begins walking together toward the lake. Cornelius and Flare duck behind some bushes as they pass. Daylight is beginning to threaten, and with the sharpness of their eyesight now, the two can just barely make it out. There's a strange man being pushed along, arms held behind his back. Where are they taking him? Who is he?

Flare looks at her brother and says, "Do you recognize him? From the outside, I mean?"

"No, I don't think so," says Cornelius.

"Was he a GUY?"

"Not sure, I couldn't see that well."

"Well, we've been here for almost two weeks," says Flare, "and this is the first time we've had an intruder. How can anyone find us, anyway?"

The thought crosses his mind, and he shoos it away. Surely not. There's no way Atlys would tell someone how to get here.

Unless she's captured. What if someone is forcing it out of her? What if it's Salem? What if it's the GU?

"Atlys knows how to get here, doesn't she?" asks Flare. "And she's still out there?"

"She wouldn't do that," says Cornelius. "No way she would do that."

"Got any better explanations?"

"Look," says Cornelius. "You don't know her the way I do. She...she saved our lives. More than once. She risked everything, just like we did. She's not capable of turning on us."

"Really?" asks Flare. "Do you not remember just last

week when she turned on all of us and was going to let us sleep outdoors? You don't remember how selfish she was?"

"Well, she did sleep outdoors this week, er, rather in the railcar and under bushes and alleys and...you just don't know what you're talking about."

Flare bristles and folds her arms tight in front of her. "I know more about Atlys than you think," she says, seething. "I had a vision of her, I'll let you know. She's a traitor. I saw her attacking Marcus and switching sides. I tried to send you the picture to warn you."

"Ha!" Cornelius throws his arms up and walks a few feet away, pacing. "You've got to be kidding me. When we were near Metrovia, she and Marcus were right outside this house when someone spotted them. It was because of Atlys' quick thinking that we all weren't killed or worse! She acted like she'd just given him a mark on his forehead. It was so believable, the guy left us alone."

"Wait, she...acted like it?"

"Yeah! Ever think you might not have the whole picture?"

"Well, I guess you do, then, right?" says Flare, hands waving in the air. "You know everything! Been everywhere, saved everyone, while I just stayed here, praying for you, praying for our parents, feeling helpless."

The silence between brother and sister grows so thick, they can almost see it like mist rising from the morning dew. The sun's coming up.

After a minute, Cornelius says, "Sorry."

"Yeah, sorry," says Flare. The two begin to walk back

to Chizoba Hall slowly. The others will surely be awake by now.

"Mom and Dad are alive," says Cornelius.

"I know," says Flare. "I look in the Book of Martyrs pretty regularly."

"Yeah, well, I didn't know, but I got pretty close to seeing them."

"Wait. Mom and Dad? You know where they are?"

"Sort of. I think they're hiding in this underground bunker. It's where we left Atlys. Her parents are supposedly hiding there, too. Mom and Dad were out though, apparently, spreading the gospel to GUYs."

"That's crazy! And dangerous! And sounds...just like them." Flare smiles and turns her head to the dark lavender sky. Then she looks at her brother. "I cannot tell you how this makes me feel. Being able to picture them, knowing they're doing okay, I just—"

"I just wanted to see them," says Cornelius. "I'd like to go back for Atlys in a day or so. Maybe they'll be there then."

"Then I'm going with you," says Flare.

"It's not up to me, it's up to Mr.—"

"I'm going. Period."

Cornelius lifts his eyebrows and lets out air. He knows enough to know there's no arguing with his sister when she's made up her mind. And as he pictures the future scene, he and Flare finding Atlys and bringing her home, he can't help but inwardly moan and pray that Atlys had nothing at all to do with this intruder. If he's honest, there's still a part of him that doesn't fully trust his new friend. But he can't tell his sister that. Can't give her that satisfaction.

~ 28 ~

The Main Hall is packed this morning. Even people who sometimes skip breakfast are here. The chatter is steady and rising as students take their seats and clink their silverware on dishes. Flare sees her whole house is here, and they're calling her over to sit with them.

"I—I'm going to sit with my house," Flare says to her brother.

Cornelius nods and finds Joe, waving at him from another table.

Amy waits for Flare to say her good mornings to everyone, then she leans in and whispers, "Where were you during the intruder alert?"

"Watching him get caught. I don't know anything more yet."

"People are saying Atlys ratted on us, and now we've been found," says Amy.

Flare looks down her table and sees lots of whispering going in. She looks over at the table where the House of Atlys is sitting, and they are doing the same thing. Does everyone think Atlys did this? Part of her feels slightly protective of her. She's not here to defend herself, anyway.

"People are also saying Cornelius and Marcus shouldn't have left her out there," says Amy.

"Well, they weren't there," says Flare. "I'm sure, knowing those two, it was the best thing to do at the time."

"Well...not sure everyone's being so understanding. If they left Atlys behind and she told the GU about Heaventree, well—"

"Amy. Please stop. All this speculation is not helpful. Let's just eat."

Flare cuts her sausage in half and eats it. But she can't stop seeing it now. All around her. People are whispering, not only about Atlys, but about her brother and Marcus, too!

She cranes her neck toward the mentors' table, but there's no one there. She's got to get some answers. Flare wipes her mouth with a napkin and sets it on the table. She stands and pushes her chair back, then goes and grabs her brother.

"Hey, I'm still eating," he says, a piece of toast dangling from his mouth.

"Bring it with you," she says. From the tone of her voice and the look on her face, Cornelius doesn't miss a beat and follows her out toward the lake.

"What are you doing?" he says, chewing and annoyed.

"We need to find out what happened. We have to know who this intruder is and how he got here."

"Well, I'm sure they'll tell us soon enough—"

"No. Corn, they—everyone's starting to turn on Atlys.

And because they think she put us in danger, they're turning on you and Marcus, too."

"What? No," he says, turning around and looking in the windows of the Main Hall. What he sees, though, isn't encouraging. All eyes are on him and Flare, staring.

Flare sees Cornelius turn bright red, so she grabs him and hauls him toward Castlebank. They need to see faculty, so that's the place to find them.

When they're almost there, Remley passes them on his way out of the building. He's in a hurry.

Flare calls to him, "Where are you going so fast?"

"Been put on special duty," he says.

"What kind of duty?"

Remley stops and thinks for a moment, or is he praying? Finally he says, "Guard duty." Then he takes off toward the lake.

"You thinking what I'm thinking?" asks Cornelius.

"Yeah," says Flare. And the two turn and trail him. He's moving faster than they've ever seen him move before. When he gets to the side of the lake, he takes a boat to the island in the center.

"The treehouse!" says Flare. "That must be where they're keeping him!"

"What in the—when was that put here?"

"This week," says Flare. "Joe worked on it. And Nattie. It's some sort of—"

"Wild architecture," he says, stunned. Is it even touching the tree? I think it's floating! How in the world did they build it so fast?"

"I don't know. Nattie helped with some special

calculations, whatever that means, but no one would say what it was for."

As the teens get closer, they are spotted by Coach Arnold. "You can't be here," he yells from in front of the treehouse. "Move along."

"But we were—"

"I mean it. This is no place for kids."

"No place for kids?" says Cornelius. "Is he kidding? Are you kidding?" he yells across the water. There is no other boat on this side of the shore. "They sent us out in a war, and now they call us kids?"

"Come on," says Flare. "It's no use. Let's just back up and watch. Maybe we'll learn something."

"Kids," says Cornelius again. If he's honest, this is the most insulted he's felt in a long time. Why? He is just a kid, isn't he? But this last week, well, he didn't feel that way. He felt like he'd aged ten years.

Don't let anyone look down on you because you are young, he hears in his spirit, *but set an example for the believers in speech, in conduct, in love, in faith and purity.* Paul's letter to Timothy floods him and helps Cornelius get on solid footing.

Yes, he's still fourteen, but he's matured a ton. Does the fact that he's still a kid mean he has no impact? Does it mean his real life will happen sometime in the future? No. His life is right now. His impact is right now. God is using Cornelius right now, this very day.

Cornelius hears a rustling and looks over in the bushes beside him. Out walks the big black dog.

"Hey, buddy," he says, calling the dog to him. He rubs his head, covered in curly black fur. "You were, like, one of the first rescues we had," he says, petting him.

"Yeah, but he doesn't belong to anyone," says Flare. "No one knows this dog. But, it acts like it's Mr. Deal's dog now. Never leaves his side, really."

"You're kidding...we, we rescued a dog that didn't need rescuing? Sheesh, what else did we do wrong?"

"That's the only one," says Flare. "Hey. If the dog is here, that means Mr. Deal must be nearby. I bet he's in the treehouse."

"If only we could get in there," says Cornelius.

"I have a better idea," says Flare. She turns to her brother with that look on her face, that determined look that is nearly impossible to deal with. "We're going to get Atlys."

"What, now?"

"Yes, now. Look, if everyone is tied up with this intruder, then they won't even miss us."

"I don't know," says Cornelius. "I would have to tell Mr. Deal. We can't just leave Heaventree."

"Are we prisoners here?"

"No, it's just that...Flare, you don't know what it's like out there."

"Well, tell me, then. I've been begging you to tell me everything." So Cornelius sits with his sister along the bank and finally tells her every single thing he saw and did on the outside. He talks for so long, the dog falls asleep next to him. When he gets to the part about the book that he brought back to Mr. Deal, he knows his sister's mind is in overdrive because she doesn't even ask him if he opened the book or not.

"We can't leave Heaventree without telling Mr. Deal," says Cornelius. And Flare doesn't fight back, doesn't say anything at all. She just puts her head on her knees and begins to cry softly. Cornelius knows she's thinking about their parents out there. He's thinking about them now, too, and lays back in the grass in the hopes he might keep his own tears from falling.

~ 29 ~

Click. Crack. "Come in, you there?"

Flare jolts. Had she fallen asleep? Where is she, anyway? She looks around and sees the water before her and the treehouse. The black dog is now gone, but her brother is passed out cold on the grass beside her.

"Amy to Flare. Come in, Flare."

Flare grabs her locket and presses. "Flare here. What's up?"

"Where are you guys? You've been gone for hours."

Flare whispers, "We're down by the treehouse. Stuck on the other side. It's where they're keeping the intruder."

"What do you mean you're stuck?" asks Amy.

"The boat that takes you to the island is over there. We don't have any way to cross the water."

The locket goes silent for a minute.

"Amy? You there? Come in."

"Joe says he knows another way to get there," says Amy. "We're on our way. Just stay put."

Cornelius is now sitting up, rubbing his eyes. "Another way? With no boat?" he asks.

Flare stands and walks around, looking for anything

she may have missed, but she sees nothing. She studies the treehouse and hears a humming.

Thrummm...thrummm...thrummm...

"Did you hear that before?" she asks her brother.

He listens and says, "I don't think so." Then he hears something else. Footsteps.

Joe and Amy round the corner and stop in front of them, panting. Obviously, they ran. "It's crazy out there," says Joe, leaning over on his knees, catching his breath.

"Yeah," says Amy, pulling her hair back into a ponytail. "It's like fear has gripped everybody. And mistrust. Now they're wondering where you are, Flare."

"What have I done?"

"You're my sister," says Cornelius. "If they don't trust me, by association, they don't trust you."

"But I don't understand."

"What's not to understand?" says Joe. "An intruder came into Heaventree. Our sense of security here is broken. Now people are afraid."

"It's spreading like fire," says Amy.

"Fear," says Cornelius, walking to the edge of the water and staring high up at the treehouse, "spreads like a virus. It just takes one to infiltrate a cell and multiply. Did you guys know the Global Union considers us a virus? Anyone without the mark?"

"Because we're spreading," says Flare. "Like what Mom and Dad are doing."

"Exactly," says Cornelius. "I think the GU is afraid of us. That's why it wants us gone. We are a greater threat than even we realize. But turning on each other...that will just weaken us."

"All right then, have no fear," says Joe. "You guys ready to get over there?"

"We have no boat," says Flare, crossing her arms.

"We don't need a boat. Check this out." Joe walks about a hundred feet to the edge of the lake. He looks around him and touches a scraggly tree next to a bush. There are markings carved in the tree. He closes his eyes and begins to murmur something. Suddenly, the water begins to stir. It sloshes from side to side and then begins to rise like a mohawk, higher in the middle.

Joe puts his foot out and steps on the water. It holds.

"You. Have. Got to be kidding me!" Cornelius grabs the back of his friend's shirt and follows, one step and then another on the water. "What is this? What did you do?"

"Shhhh," says Joe. "Just keep moving."

When all four teens have stepped onto the island, the water plummets and spreads out in ripples as if nothing strange had just happened.

"A water bridge?" asks Cornelius, freaking out. "Dude, we just walked on water!"

"Like Jesus," says Amy, stunned.

"Not like Jesus," says Joe, "with Jesus. It's a failsafe for believers. A hidden bridge placed there that only we can use. A non-believer would never know about it—"

"And even if they did," says Flare, understanding, "they couldn't pray to the Lord and walk with Him?"

"Exactly," says Joe. "Now. Ready to go inside?"

Thrummm...thrummm...thrummm...

"The humming is even louder over here," says Flare. The teens tiptoe along the underbrush of the tree, trying not to make a sound. When they come around to the front, they freeze. There, hanging in midair, swinging a glowing sword back and forth in front of them is...

"Mister Remley!" says Flare.

But he doesn't seem to hear them. It's as if he's here, but not here, his eyes cast straight ahead.

"After he drove the man out," says Cornelius, quoting Genesis 3:21, "he placed on the east side of the Garden of Eden cherubim and a flaming sword flashing back and forth to guard the way of the tree of life."

"But this can't be the tree of life," says Flare, "because they put the intruder in there."

"It's more like a prison," says Joe.

"Yeah," says Cornelius, "like Alcatraz, the old prison on an island near San Francisco. Only one way on and no way off. I—"

"What in the world are you doing over here?" It's Mr. Deal's voice. "Cornelius Flanagan."

Cornelius turns. "Sir, I—"

"It's my fault, sir," says Joe, stepping forward. "I brought them over. We...wanted to know more about the intruder."

Mr. Deal adjusts his cap and takes a deep breath. "You do know, do you not, that I would inform you students as soon as I could, as soon as you needed to know."

"We do, it's just—" Flare tucks a red lock of hair behind her ear. She scratches the outside of her cast as if she can feel it. "With Atlys still outside and the intruder coming in..."

"Go on," says Mr. Deal, crossing his arms and looking at the ground. "I'm listening."

"Well, it appears everybody is starting to suspect Atlys had something to do with it. And...so now they're turning on Cornelius and Marcus—"

"And now Flare," says Cornelius.

"And so let me get this straight," says Mr. Deal. "You and your sister are heads of two of the houses at Heaventree. There are 24 people in each house..." He pretends to count on his fingers. "That means 48 students have no leadership right now. No, with Atlys gone, that's...a whopping 72 students or half the population of this school! Now, let me ask you, as heads of houses, is there something you ought to be doing right now?"

"Sir, we wanted to go back to them with answers."

"Answers," says Mr. Deal. "Mister Flanagan, do you know how many times we have to face difficult pressures in life without any answers? Sometimes you have to go with the little you've been given. By faith. That is precisely what you need to be doing now."

"Well, can you tell us anything at all?" says Flare. "Is he a GUY?"

Mr. Deal gets still. "He is."

"And do you know how he found this place?"

"At this time, we do not."

"So it could be Atlys," says Amy.

"It could be, but that doesn't mean it is. That is but one small possibility. And so, you four are going to go back to your houses immediately and put a stop to this gossip before it gets out of control."

The kids are silent and watch Remley's sword flashing left and right, left and right, *thrummm...thrummm...thrummm...*

"Leave now," says Mr. Deal, the sound of his voice leaving no room for questions or conversations.

Dutifully, but with their tails between their legs, the teens turn and head toward the edge of the water. "Not that way," says Mr. Deal. "The bridge is only to be used in emergencies. Miss Flanagan, please get in." And all four teens crawl into the boat with Mr. Deal at the helm. They're going back to face what awaits them. As the wind blows Flare's hair behind her, she wonders how they can stop the spread of fear when it has gripped their entire school?

As if he was reading her mind, Cornelius says, "Perfect love. It casts out fear."

~ 30 ~

The boat hits the shore and Cornelius, Amy, Flare and Joe begin to step out. The black dog is wagging its tail, happy to see Mr. Deal. "There you are, dog. Cannot go anywhere without this dog. What is it about me? Hmm? Haven't you figured out I don't like dogs? Don't like animals at all?"

"I don't think it believes you," says Cornelius, laughing.

"Mr. Deal," says Amy, while he pulls the boat ashore. "Why couldn't someone just swim across this lake and get to the island?"

Mr. Deal stops and looks her squarely in the eyes. He raises his eyebrows. "Whew," he exhales. "I would not advise that."

"Why? It's just water, right?"

"Just water? Maybe," says Mr. Deal. "But what's in the water? Best you not find out."

The teens stare out over the water and look for anything ominous. Sea creatures. Monsters. Snakes. Whatever it is, it's enough to move Joe a few feet back from the water...just in case.

But curiosity gets the best of Cornelius, and he grabs a stick and hurls it out into the water.

Swoosh!

The black dog hurtles past him and jumps out into the water, swimming toward the stick.

"No!" says Cornelius! "Oh no, please boy, come back!"

"Come back, come back!" they all yell. Mr. Deal stands silent as they watch the dog grab the stick and come paddling back to the shore.

"Come on, boy," says Flare. The dog makes it and seems pleased with himself. He drops the stick and shakes water all over everyone.

"You had us so scared!" says Joe. "I thought you couldn't swim in that water. Mr. Deal?"

But Mr. Deal has already turned and begun walking quickly back to the buildings. The big wet dog gallups right next to him every step of the way.

Cornelius runs to catch up with him. "Sir? Sir, did you hear Joe back there?"

Mr. Deal doesn't say a word.

"Come on, you have to tell us what you meant. If the dog could swim—"

Mr. Deal stops abruptly and turns to glare at Cornelius. The dog stops and scratches its side with a hind leg. Slowly, but unmistakingly, Mr. Deal lowers his eyes to the dog, then lifts his hat, touching his scar. He slowly looks back down at the dog.

And then Cornelius sees it. With the hair wet on its head, it's easy to see it now. Cornelius' eyes grow large.

"I'm not feeling very well, Cornelius," Mr. Deal says slowly. "Would you...escort me to the infirmary, so I might get...looked at?"

"Oh, yes, of course," he says. Cornelius covers his mouth and follows Mr. Deal with the dog by his side every step of the way. When Joe, Flare and Amy catch up, Cornelius shoos them away.

"Look, I—I'm going to take Mr. Deal to the infirmary. I'll catch up with you guys soon."

"Infirmary," says Amy. "Are you all right?"

"We'll catch up soon." Cornelius eyes his sister and conveys to her that he knows more than he's saying.

"Got it," says Flare. "Let's go, guys." And they take off toward the houses of Heaventree.

"Wait here just a minute," Mr. Deal says to Cornelius when they reach the entrance of the infirmary. The dog pants and sits next to him.

"Sure," says Cornelius, "we'll wait right here." Left with the dog, Cornelius looks around him. He replays that first day outside of Heaventree in his head. He remembers exactly where he was when this dog started trailing them. Atlys had insisted they help the dog.

Atlys. Cornelius feels sick. Maybe he'll need to be "looked at" next.

In an instant, Mr. Deal is standing at the glass door, looking at the dog, and a nurse comes up beside him. "Oh, I just love dogs," she says to him. "Is he yours? Can I pet him?"

She opens the door and comes out to the black dog who

wags his tail all the harder. She pets his head and quickly touches the chip. Then she says how handsome he is and then suddenly—

The black dog falls to the ground.

The nurse puts a cap on the syringe she was holding and says, "Quick, grab his hind legs. It might take three of us, and we have to work quickly."

The three haul the dog indoors and into a small sterile room. A doctor is waiting there for them. "I don't usually work on animals," she says, "but there's a first for everything."

After a few minutes, the doctor says, "It's out." She drops the chip into a metal bowl. Then she uses a needle and thread to stitch up the dog's forehead. "Who would do this to an animal?"

"Not who, but what," says Mr. Deal. "I'm afraid he isn't the only one. Poor, stupid dog."

"Wait, you said this dog has been following you around all week?" says Cornelius. "Wouldn't leave your side?"

"You know it."

"Then it wasn't Atlys," says Cornelius.

"I would...say her chances of being cleared of any wrongdoing are extremely high at this point," he admits.

"Then we have to go get her. Send me. I'm ready. And my sister wants to go too."

"Oooh, I'm afraid that's a no can-do."

"Why not?! You said it yourself, Atlys is innocent. So we need to go get her!"

"I'm afraid I cannot send you out to get her...because arrangements are already being made as we speak."

"Sorry to interrupt, but your dog is going to be super groggy when he wakes up," says the doctor. "And if he's been under the control of this mark of the GU, he may be completely disoriented or scared or maybe fine. I've seen humans when they have theirs removed, but animals, that's a different story. I honestly don't know how he will react."

"Mister Flanagan, here, will be more than happy to watch the dog while it wakes up."

"But—"

"If you'll excuse me, then, gentlemen, I will get ready for the next extraction." And with that, the doctor leaves the room. Cornelius and Mr. Deal are left standing over the black dog. His chest is barely moving, but he is breathing.

"Poor, stupid dog," says Mr. Deal. "And to think I thought you actually liked me. Looks like you were only spying on us here." He's quiet, obviously thinking of all the things the dog may have conveyed to the outside world. The location of Heaventree, for instance.

"So who's looking for Atlys?" asks Cornelius. He's pouting a little. He wanted to be the one to bring her home. Hoped he could see his parents at the same time.

"Someone who has no ties to the outside world, no living parents with which to be swayed."

"But sir, Atlys made a good point. Why can't we let our parents come here? Why can't we bring the believers here?"

"Why, indeed," says Mr. Deal. "It's something I've asked the Lord a thousand times. And you know what his answer has been? Silence on the matter. And so, I keep going without answers."

"By faith," says Cornelius.

"Yes, by faith. When our friend, here, wakes up, walk him over to the House of Josh. He can care for him there. And then join me in a town meeting of sorts. I believe we have some things to clear up with the students of Heaventree."

"I will," says Cornelius. "But, sir?"

Mr. Deal turns.

"The doctor said 'the next extraction.' Did she mean—"

"The treehouse? Yes, she's headed there now."

Mr. Deal walks out, and Cornelius thinks he sees him walk a little more stooped over, as if the weight of the world is bearing down on him. The strain of having to protect all these kids and animals is starting to show. Cornelius looks at the dog and wonders what else the Global Union knows about Heaventree. Is it even safe here anymore? Is anywhere safe?

~ 31 ~

The whole student body of Heaventree has been assembled in the Main Hall, once again, but this time under the ruse of a smoothie and boba tea bar. It's midafternoon, and Flare has yet to assemble her creatives for their daily session to protect the dome. She makes a mental note to let everyone know it will take place just after this.

Whatever this is.

Mr. Deal had used the loudspeaker to call everyone in, but she hasn't seen Cornelius yet. Nor Amy. Instead of worrying, she's going to trust just this time.

"Friends, neighbors, countrymen," begins Mr. Deal, standing and clinking the glass of his smoothie. "Thank you all for gathering here today. I do hope you're enjoying your smoothies?"

Half the room erupts.

"And for those of you who are not so smooth...boba tea!"

The other half cheers and claps.

"Good. Now, I know you all heard the unmistakable intruder alert this morning. Good news is, it works. The not so good news is...well, we have an intruder on the premises."

A murmur takes over the crowd.

"However, the even better news is that the suspect is in our custody and under control." He sets his glass down and asks Madame Dubose to watch it for him, and people giggle at the look on her face. "Now, it has come to my attention that some of you are questioning how someone found out about Heaventree. It is not as if we advertise. In fact, we work extremely hard to remain hidden here. For your safety. So how did the perpetrator find us hidden here? Anyone?"

"Atlys!" yells a boy in Josh's house.

"And you would be wrong," says Mr. Deal, smiling. "Atlys had nothing to do with this. The sad truth of the matter is...oh, here he is now. Mister Flanagan, would you join me, sir?"

"Sir?"

Flare nearly coughs up her boba tea. Is he hanging her brother out to dry?

Dutifully but cautiously, Cornelius begins to walk toward his mentor. When he's at his side, Mr. Deal places his arm around him. "Cornelius Flanagan, House of Cornelius, how are you today."

"Fine, sir."

"Have you learned anything today that may shed some light on how, in fact, a strange GUY—and yes, he's a GUY, everyone—how someone like him might find his way to and inside Heaventree?"

"Yes sir," says Cornelius. Flare stands to her feet, ready

for whatever is coming. "There's a dog, sir, a black dog, that had a chip. It had the mark."

"You mean to tell me that a dog has been spying on us all along? That it is not our fearless leader, Atlys, who remains on the outside at the moment, and instead a mangy mutt that has put us all in danger?"

"Seems so," says Cornelius. "We-we didn't know though. We didn't know it had the mark. It was an honest mistake."

"An honest mistake, indeed," says Mr. Deal. "In fact, I've had this creature by my side all week— and I don't mean to brag, but I am a bit of an expert at these things— and this dog, well, it snowed me too."

The room grumbles and then grows very quiet.

"Do not forget, friends, that we are the House of Heaventree, not the houses. We are the body of Christ. We are full of grace in our thoughts and conversations about one another. And when in doubt, we do not gossip but take our petition to the Lord...or to me." Mr. Deal walks to Cornelius' side and calls Marcus up as well. He places his hands on both of their shoulders from behind and says, "I think it's about time these two were welcomed home like the heroes they are. Please, everyone. Join me in saying 'a job well done.'"

The room erupts in cheers. Maybe it's the sugar, but Flare feels the celebration in her cheeks. Yes, this is the way it's supposed to be. One house. One body. One faith.

But suddenly the cheers change to screaming and chaos. What was that, an earthquake? A bomb? Everything is shaken, and no drink is left upright on the tables.

Flare is on the floor, grabbing the leg of her chair, and if she's honest, hiding.

Mr. Deal grabs Cornelius and Joe. They run to Flare and he yells, "You three, follow me!"

People are beginning to scramble for the exits, but Mr. Deal leads them down a hallway near the kitchen. They keep running until they see Castlebank looming over them. The sky is beginning to grow dark. "Wait here!" says Mr. Deal as he runs into the building.

Flare begins to pray silently, and soon she knows it. There's a hole in the protective dome. Something's wrong.

"Wait here!" she says as she runs back to Chizoba Hall for her art supplies.

But the boys don't wait there. As soon as she runs down the stairwell, she's greeted by her brother, Joe and Mr. Deal. "Well, let's go!" he yells. "No time to waste!"

There is smoke billowing at the top of the treehouse, dark blue and angry swirls.

"Joe," says Mr. Deal, stopping just short of the shore and panting. "You helped build this structure."

"I did, sir."

"And so you know how to get to the very top. I mean, the absolute top. There's a lever and a hatch—"

"I know it, sir. I placed it there."

"Joe, I need you to get these two up there. No matter what. Immediately." Mr. Deal turns his attention to Flare. He touches her arm. "We've been breached. This is serious. The dome is failing. Joe will get you as close as he can."

"Okay, I-I'll do my best. But, oh my gosh—"

"And you," says Mr. Deal to Cornelius. "I know you

put yourself in grave danger already, and I thank you. And I know you protected the book that Mr. Chang gave you to give to me. Do you remember what he said about opening it?"

Cornelius thinks for a second. "He said it was to be opened at the correct time by the correct one. Is now the time?"

Mr. Deal reaches in his jacket and pulls out the twine-wrapped package.

"Now is the time," he says. He unties the twine and slowly pulls the brown paper off. It slides to the grass, and a dark gray, ancient book is left in his hands. It's sealed with blue wax and strange markings, almost like those on the tree by the water bridge.

Cornelius eagerly awaits the opening of the book and is stunned when Mr. Deal pushes it in his direction.

"Wait. What? Aren't you going to open it?" asks Cornelius, beginning to panic.

"I'm not the one," says Mr. Deal. "You are. Now take it to the top of the treehouse. You guys get as close as you can to the dome. Flare will work on mending it, but I'm afraid there is much more coming our way. You guys are our only hope."

"But—"

"No time for buts, Cornelius. Take the water bridge...it's faster, and if ever there was an emergency, this is it. I'll follow you up and check in on our intruder."

Joe touches the tree and they all begin praying. The water swells so quickly and so tall, it nearly hurls them over to the island.

~ 32 ~

Thrummm...thrummm...thrummm...

"Remley, let us pass," says Mr. Deal, and for a moment the sword is put aside. As they begin crawling up the tree, the sword begins to flash again.

Up and up they climb, a little awkward with Flare's lower arm cast, but they soon make it to a landing with stairs. Up and up they go, higher and higher. How big is this place, anyway? Mr. Deal stops them at the fifteenth floor and tells them all to keep going up the stairs as he opens it. It sounds as if a fight is going on in the room behind it. Suddenly the treehouse shakes again, and everyone tumbles a few steps back. A wind begins to fill the staircase like a howling train, and everyone's hair is standing straight up. Mr. Deal's cap flies off.

"This is my stop!" yells Mr. Deal.

Joe points to the scar on his forehead and says, "What the—"

"We know," says Cornelius. "It's a long story. We'll tell you later!"

"Keep going!" screams Mr. Deal. "Follow Joe, and whatever you do, pray, pray, pray while you do it. Cornelius, the book you're holding is the Book of Reflection. Remember all the times God confused the enemy so they turned on themselves?"

"I remember, sir!"

"Good, just don't look into the book yourself. The reflection magnifies one-hundredfold, whether love or hate or envy or pride..."

"Sir, that's why Salem wanted the book?"

"That's why Salem should never have the book. He would fall like Narcissus. Now go on you guys! And remember—you are loved and you are worthy. And right now, you're all we've got!"

The door slams behind him, and the three teens spiral higher into the windy staircase, forced to hold on to the railing now, Flare clutching her sketchbook under her cast and Cornelius carrying the Book of Reflection. *Please God,* he's praying, *let me know what to do and when to do it. Fill my head with your wisdom and—*

"We're here!" Joe pushes a large lever and a hatch opens up to smoke and fire above them. Before he has time to be afraid, Cornelius crawls through and gasps for air.

So it's all come down to this, he thinks. Cornelius looks around him. From way up here he should be afraid of heights. The buildings of Heaventree look like anthills, but worse than that is what's beyond. Usually, the sky of Heaventree looks peaceful or rainy or...normal. But now, the sky is furious and twists with smoke and trails of...bombs? Missiles?

"Get up here!" He says to his sister, and a red swirl of hair emerges, the wind whipping at her face. Cornelius keeps his footing and helps Flare climb up.

"It's worse that I thought!" she screams. "We can actually see the outside!"

There are a few tree branches that reach up higher into the air, and Flare gauges her steps. Can she make it? One, two, three! Flare jumps to the tree branch and wraps her arms and legs around it. Then she pulls out her sketchbook and grabs a pencil from her pocket. "I don't know if I can do this!" she yells.

"You have to try!" says Cornelius. "I can do all things through Christ who strengthens me. Remember?"

Flare closes her eyes and grips the branch harder with her legs. It's swaying, and she can't afford to fall. She begins to picture the break in the dome and can see it in her mind's eye. So she begins to move her pencil over the paper. Over and over, around and up, she has no idea what she's drawing, but she trusts it's what should be drawn. Her eyes open just once to see her brother crawling up another tree branch even higher than hers.

It's more than she can bear. *Please God, keep him safe. Please keep us safe, protect Heaventree, cover us with your protection—*

Suddenly, Cornelius stops and stares straight up. Is he seeing an angel? Seeing the face of God? What?

"Bombs! More than I can count!" he screams. "Coming right at us!"

"Do something!"

Duck and hide is what Cornelius feels like doing, but instead, he breaks the seal of the Book of Reflection. With his free hand, he opens the book and hurls it up into the air above him. Then, nothing happens. No bomb, no shaking.

"You're doing it!" yells Flare.

"Doing what?!"

"I don't know, but whatever it is, it's working!"

Cornelius looks up and sees a beam of light flowing from the book and out of Heaventree. Suddenly, they hear the unmistakeable sound of bombs falling...but they're not falling on Heaventree.

"They're bombing themselves!" squeals Flare. "Keep it up, Corn!"

Cornelius' arm is getting tired, but he grits his teeth and lifts the book higher.

Flare turns the page of her sketchbook and draws some more, praying all the while, and when the beam of light fades, the sky above them turns blue again. The wind has stopped, and Cornelius and his sister stare at each other in disbelief.

"You... did it," says Cornelius. "You healed the dome!"

"You did it!" she says, smiling. "You confused the enemy and made it turn on itself!"

When Flare begins to crawl down the branch she notices Joe's head peeking out of the hatch. His eyes are wide and his mouth is dropped open. His hair, like the rest of them, is sticking out in all directions. "You okay, Joe?"

He nods, barely, but can't speak.

As they head back down the stairway, Joe is beginning to find his voice. "I cannot believe what I just saw. Cannot believe it! Wait until they hear about this!"

"Hear about what?" says a familiar voice. Mr. Deal emerges behind them from the doorway of level 15. His jacket is ripped, and his hat is crooked.

"They did it!" says Joe. " I saw it with my own eyes! She scribbled in this book, and he held a book over his head and—"

"And we are safe again," says Mr. Deal. "Thank you, Lord, we are safe again."

"What about the intruder?" asks Flare, motioning to the door behind them.

"He...won't be giving us any more trouble," says Mr. Deal. "I tell you, that was one tough chip to remove, though." He scrunches his face. "Deep. So...embedded. It was apparent he'd been a GUY for life. He admitted he'd been a child when he was marked. Like I was. Had no choice in the matter. We're going to help him rehabilitate, if that's what you call it. Give him some time to think clearly."

"Learning to live again," says Flare.

"Really, for the first time, yes. But we can't keep him here. He'll be heading out into the field. He will join the many other converts who are doing the hard work of learning to think for themselves, finding out who they truly are and what they're here for."

The group walks down the stairs, exhausted, minds whirling. At the next level down, Flare stops. "Mr. Deal?"

He gives her his attention.

"The damage to the dome was just above this treehouse. Was the GUY sending out signals to the GU? Is that how they knew where to attack us?"

"Interesting you should ask," he says. "This treehouse was built to extinguish any of the GU signals. It's impossible to transmit from here."

"But then, how were we able to get high enough to the precise place we would need to be in order to save Heaventree?"

Mr. Deal comes close to Flare and smoothes out her frazzled red hair, resting his hands on her shoulders. "You do realize this is where the Lord told me to build the treehouse, correct? You realize he told me how to build it, the dimensions, everything. When will you people understand this is all about Jesus? Every bit. He is the one preparing and protecting us. This is all him." Flare's eyes fill with understanding. And awe. And her mind is blown even more than it was a moment ago. She sees her place in God's purpose, and it's humbling.

~ 33 ~

When they get outside the treehouse and pass Remley's sword, Flare picks up her locket. "Amy? Come in. Can you hear me?"

She doesn't hear anything. "Amy? Come in. It's me."

Mr. Deal is stepping onto the boat and beckoning them all to climb in. "Pretty sure she can't hear you," he says.

"Who?" says Flare. "Amy? Why?"

Mr. Deal straightens his cap and sniffs. "Amy's been sent to gather Atlys for us."

"What do you mean?" asks Cornelius? His heart rate was just slowing down to normal, but now it's pounding again. "You sent Amy out there? Are you... nuts?!"

"Mister Flanagan, I—"

"No, send me instead!" Cornelius screams. "She's too sweet! And sensitive, and—and if anything happens to her—"

Flare looks at her brother and touches his rigid back. It's obvious how much he cares for Amy.

"Did she go alone?" asks Flare, trying to bring a level head to the conversation.

"Marcus is with her."

"Oh, great, Marcus, who's injured—" whines Cornelius.

"Enough," says Mr. Deal. "Why, Lord, did you have me work with children?"

"Children?" says Cornelius, incensed. "You just sent those children out into a warzone!"

"Do. You. Have. No faith yet?" Mr. Deal turns and starts the engine. When they get back to the shore, he pulls the boat up and the black dog comes running to him, wagging his tail and licking his face. He nearly knocks him over.

Flare notices the tears in Mr. Deal's eyes. "You do love me, don't you, boy? You might be the only one."

Mr. Deal stands and turns to face Joe, Cornelius and Flare. His face is red. After what just happened up there, they should all be celebrating, but instead, Mr. Deal just looks weary. He turns and slowly walks away as if anvils are tied to his feet. The curly black dog keeps his pace.

"Do you have to question everything he does?" asks Flare, when he's safely out of earshot.

"Me? You question him all the time!" says Cornelius.

"Yeah, but look at what just happened," she says. "He saved Heaventree."

"We saved Heaventree."

"To be fair," says Joe, chiming in, "if it weren't for Mr. Deal obeying Jesus, neither one of you could do what you just did. And if it weren't for me, you wouldn't have known the way. So, really, you both ought to be thanking me."

Cornelius pushes his friend a few feet, nearly toppling him, then they head back toward the Houses of Heaventree. Flare is dying to see Josh and make sure he's okay. She can't wait to tell him what happened.

But Cornelius never knew how much he cared about Amy until this very moment. And he cares so much, it scares him. He holds the Book of Reflection in his hands and realizes he should have given it back to Mr. Deal. Heaven forbid Cornelius look directly into the book. Who knows what he would see? What pathetic part of him would be magnified one-hundredfold? Fear? Insecurity?

Or love?

As if reading his mind, Flare takes her brother's arm in hers and whispers, "Perfect love casts out fear, remember? I'm sure Amy and Marcus will be fine. But I know a place where we can find out for sure."

So the three head off toward Castlebank, toward the Book of Martyrs, praying along the way that no one they know will be written there.

When Mr. Deal and his dog arrive in his room at Castlebank, he considers that it might be nice having a companion for once. "You're the only one that understands me," he says. Mr. Deal takes his shoes off and lies back on his bed, completely worn out. The dog jumps up and lays at his feet. A dog at his feet. So quaint. He never got to have a dog. Never got to have a childhood like the other kids who didn't have the mark. Never got to have a wife...or kids.

And suddenly, he understands just a little. At Heaventree he's surrounded by pets and children. Is this not what the Lord prepared for him?

"Oh, thank you, God, for your love. I do not deserve it, and yet, I'm so grateful. You know me so well. Help me to be what these children need me to be."

"He-hell-o?"

A scratchy noise comes from his old transistor radio on the desk. He gets up to grab it.

"Hello?" the voice sounds again. *Crack.*

"Hello, who is this?" says Mr. Deal, pressing down the button.

"It's Amy. Mr. Deal?"

"Amy, oh, thank God. It works. Are you okay? Did you find Atlys?"

"We're okay," she says, "Marcus and me, but...there's been an earthquake or something." *Crack.* "The house Marcus says they entered has been destroyed. There's... no way down there."

Mr. Deal pulls his cap back on. "Stay put!" he says. "No, scratch that. Stay hidden, and abort this mission. I need you two to come back home. Now."

There is quiet for a moment. "Amy? Amy, do you read me?"

"We'll find a way in," she says. "We're not leaving until we find Atlys."

"That was not a suggestion, Miss Feinstein, that was an order."

Click. Click. "Amy? Amy, come in."

But there is nothing but static. And the sound of it forces Mr. Deal to his knees.

Please, Lord, watch over them. Protect the House of Heaventree, and Lord, forgive me for putting these children in danger.

When he stands up, Mr. Deal's face settles from anguish into something more like peace. Or resolve. He understands now that the game has changed. The stakes have gotten higher.

The seal has been broken, and there's no turning back now.

"Your will be done," he says to his maker as he pulls on his shoes. Then he heads out to hold a secret mentors' meeting. His friends need to know about and to help plan the next phase.

Because it won't be easy. Or safe. But there's no doubt in his mind what the Lord is asking him to do now.

It's time to bring home the remnant.

ABOUT THE AUTHOR

The Virus is Nicole Seitz' second YA novel, Book 2 in the *House of Heaventree* series. Seitz is the acclaimed author of seven other adult novels and two non-fiction anthologies. She teaches visual art, creative writing and illustration at a school in the Charleston, SC area where she lives with her husband and two children. Seitz is a graduate of the University of North Carolina at Chapel Hill's School of Journalism and also has a degree in Illustration from Savannah College of Art & Design. Her paintings are featured on the covers of her books. Visit her web site at www.nicoleseitz.com for more information.

ALSO BY NICOLE SEITZ

YA Fiction

The Firstborn (House of Heaventree, Book 1 - Stay tuned for Book 3!)

Adult Fiction

The Cage-maker
Beyond Molasses Creek
The Inheritance of Beauty
Saving Cicadas
A Hundred Years of Happiness
Trouble the Water
The Spirit of Sweetgrass

Adult Non-fiction

When You Pass Through Waters: Words of Hope and Healing from Your Favorite Authors
Our Prince of Scribes: Writers Remember Pat Conroy (coeditor)

www.ingramcontent.com/pod-product-compliance
Lightning Source LLC
LaVergne TN
LVHW041945070526
838199LV00051BA/2906